ORLEANS PARISH

ORLEANS
PARISH

ORLEANS PARISH

A NOVEL

CHAD PENTLER

atmosphere press

CARSON

2022

FATHER HANDS ME money. He drops a stack of crisp greenbacks in my hand, telling me, "Go to Los Angeles. Fulfill those dreams of yours if it's really what you want— if LA is *really* how you see yourself." He motivates and dismisses at the same time, his throaty timbre unencumbered by any trace of indecision. Let's be real, though. He's not the one who needs to make the decision. In his own life, he postures like a three-point shooter who doesn't follow through. The man sheds pieces of his fruitless dreams wherever he goes; it's the cost he weathers in order to remain with my mother, Moira, a woman who chuckles in the face of obstinate obstructions. I consider Father's unintentional dare to head west each time I reflect on the risk I've undertaken here in Los Angeles. He doesn't know what it means to want what I want. Too late for him to make the connection. So I trade the humidity, the swamp, and my mother's whispers of special abilities and the potential for a higher calling for something of far less substance: a serene ocean breeze as soothing as a neck massage. I trade Orleans Parish and all it could offer away for the far-off chance of screenwriting success. Because Father doles out money—and also makes a large deposit in my savings account. This detail is there in the background whenever I order eggs Benedict at that little place on Montana Avenue with the white table cloths and the perky waitress who surfed before work. She dreams of trading her regional theater credits for a coveted TV pilot that materializes out of the ether because some newly minted lower-level executive liked a writer's idea about a female cop who patrols the Alaskan wilderness the day before a pivotal presidential election featuring the home state senator. That pilot. The one the writer came up with on a bouncy Uber ride on the way to a meeting with a family connection the week before the artificial deadline she gave herself—before it was time to drive back to Scottsdale, Arizona...or Waltham, Massachusetts...or Urbana, Illinois. Or Orleans Parish. The deadline I would have conjured myself if I wasn't so afraid of my subconscious.

No deadline is set for me to return home. I suspect a deadline lurks anyway behind the black Land Rover in the claustrophobic traffic jam at the corner of Barrington Avenue and San Vicente, which isn't a traffic jam: just Tuesday. The deadline might be hiding behind the amorphous rock mound I sit atop, enjoying a glimmering view of Venice Beach as I hear about the local goings-on from my actor friend from film school, the one who actually snagged a television pilot (to act in) with a full season order practically as soon as he arrived because he was more talented than the others, but also because his smile disarmed multiple executives, and they, in turn, wanted to spread this warmhearted, reassuring grin as wide and as far as they possibly could from Cedarburg, Wisconsin to Mount Lebanon, Pennsylvania and into their savings accounts—direct deposit.

Some deadline is real, a looming end game and tangible panic lurking at the back of one's throat. Nearly everyone contemplates the panic because if you do not contemplate it, if you pretend you're here for good when you haven't earned a thing, you could wake up one morning, look in the mirror, and see a washed-up, bitter forty-year-old with a paunch and decaying teeth staring back at you. Happens here every day.

When there is a deadline, you make compromises, small and smaller still—sooner rather than later. The first one is to work for free at a production company. The theory: get your foot in the door; obtain a job second. These two theories should coalesce around a single remedy. Unfortunately, they do not. Find myself in an open space with upbeat sea-green walls alongside the soothing presence of familiar movie posters, all from films I've seen (and liked). The posters exhibit confidence. The sniping assistants project indifference. The assistants are not paid much more than I would be paid (nothing) even though they participate in an intricate system of emails, phone calls, errands in the car, and sometimes luncheons, all contributing to the system, which would collapse without their expert stewardship. The system thrives on spreading feelings of inadequacy to anyone finding themselves lower on the totem pole. The executives make the assistants feel deficient. The assistants make the interns feel defective. The interns do not search for moments of triumph but instead for glimmers of competency, which temporarily ameliorates their sense of inadequacy. The interns and the assistants are, to be sure, easily replaceable, but the executives would prefer to keep them working in a stalemate for as long as possible. Occasionally, when someone does leave, those same bosses must maintain their composure even though their control of the system and, consequently, their livelihood plummets toward real jeopardy until they secure the next so-called "irreplaceable assistant"—the one they will rave about to their colleagues—while they simultaneously entertain the possibility of sleeping with that same assistant because they can and will get away with it. The executives are architects stretching their creativity among a fledgling city. In the world the executives construct from their dreams, putting projects together is its own reward except when it isn't, which is when they secure their percentage.

I attempt to join the system because I perceive no other options. I need to join the system because the city is a giant fishing net ensnaring all possible inroads to a future I envisioned when I was little. The one where I write the Oscar-winning film and thank everyone who shunned me in high school. Must locate a tear in the fishing net.

So when I sit for my interview at this production company with sea-green shaded walls and marquee movie posters, I talk about being trapped in the hurricane with my brother: the worst hurricane of the first quarter of the 21st century.

On the other side of the dull, yellow-hued, leather Pottery Barn couch sits a newly minted late-twenty-something executive who only ascended the corporate ladder of the intricate system one month earlier. I tell the executive the hurricane is what drove me to begin writing, but I was never *only* interested in writing. I also wanted to create films from the ground up. Doesn't everyone here? It sure sounds promising when you say it out loud.

She looks on with wry amusement at the details I describe: being trapped in my high school with my overenthusiastic brother. Waiting for our parents to arrive via motor boat. The deafening realization something may have happened to them. That no organized rescue was on the way. Maybe she's calculating how much it would cost to green light a project based on the story I indirectly pitch to her. I suspect she would take credit for the idea. I only want the internship.

The newly minted executive does her best impression of detached skepticism inherent only in more experienced, older executives. Her skepticism unfortunately metastasizes into a cold concoction of superiority and light indifference. I wish to impress her all the more, completely forgetting the detail that the internship is not for pay. No participant in the system would ever admit this no-pay detail could be a reasonable pretext to dissuade a potential applicant.

"Where do you see yourself in five years?" she asks, the last of her likely mandatory questions but the first from her end that could truly reveal something.

"Watching the second film I've written and produced. In the movie theater," I add as an afterthought. I need my reply to initiate a real conversation, but from the moment I arrive in the city, I'm stripped of the ability to make true connections with people. It's like every person in the business wears a deflector shield shrouding them in a cold but necessary disposition. Never had this problem in school or Uptown at home.

The woman straightens in her chair, picking up on a fact I uttered a minute ago. "Wait, you have a B.F.A.?" She says the name of my school out loud, as if sounding out the phonemes of the familiar university in New York City makes the credential less impressive.

"I was hoping you could help me find an assistant job on a TV show or as an assistant to a movie producer once the internship finishes," I say. I glance at her arm muscles. They're substantial. When does she have the time to work out like that? If Sebastian were here, he'd note how she appears to have lost some femininity from heightened exercise. I disagree.

Her lips slip into a smile as she decides my fate. She parts her hand through her thick auburn hair. "Your script coverage is top notch. The best from a *potential* intern I've ever seen. We don't usually hire someone with your experience." Her language is confounding. If I'm that impressive, isn't there some kind of real job they can offer? Can you really hire someone with no plans to pay them?

"Can you think of any jobs with a salary I would qualify for?" I actually ask despite the risk. "Your production company produced so many films I've enjoyed over the years. I'd love to be a part of it." This sounds so trite. *I'd love to be a part of it*—like I'm talking to some U-10 soccer coach when I was younger. Some people need to feel the same impression in a different light. I try to shine some her way, but it's frigid and dreary in the air-conditioned office. Did she turn the air conditioning up on purpose?

"We don't usually hire an assistant before they're an intern first."

"Right, but you said I'm too experienced to be an

intern."

"Your experience from your film school studies will make you a valuable member of our intern team. I'm sure there will be opportunity for advancement down the line."

"Okay," I say, relieved for once I said all I could. "Let's begin."

At 8:30 the following Monday, the lobby of the production company is as vacant as the inside of a restaurant during a pandemic. The executives and assistants are not in the office yet, but Helena, a methodical woman in charge of the interns whose business air suggests more finance than film, hands me a debit card for my first errand: breakfast—for them, not me. She hands me a print-out with five breakfast orders.

"Give them this along with the debit card. The restaurant's in the lobby. Not bad for your first trip," she says. I agree. "Also, make sure the eggs are runny. If they're not, I'll have to send you back."

I stand in the empty elevator, already jumpy about the breakfast. I understand the desire for runny eggs; I prefer my own eggs the same way, but I will not be cooking those eggs. Do they want me to supervise the cooking of the eggs? Where are the other interns? The elevator door slides open.

The restaurant is almost as quiet as the production company: no line to order. Only a few young professionals sit along the window reading the trades on their iPads. At the counter, I pass the order and the debit card to the waitress. I remind her about the runny eggs. She looks at me like I've just asked where California is. "Wait by the tables," she says. No one likes to be told how to do their jobs, especially from complete novices like me. I suspect the entire town depends on novices reminding experienced professionals how to do their jobs as long as those experienced professionals aren't executives. Once I'm summoned back to the counter, the waitress provides me with a plastic tote bag filled with the five breakfast boxes. "They're runny," she says with a wink.

My appreciation swells. "Thank you."

Upon my return, Helena takes the bag from me with a grunt. "Before long it will be lunch time," she says.

Lunch time is way off. I notice only a third of the assistants are at their computers. "Runny eggs," I add.

She nods, unimpressed.

Half-partitions form a barrier between each cubicle. Helena leads me past the cubicles and into an empty conference room with opened laptops set up at each seat: seven in all.

"Am I the only intern here today?" I ask.

"There should be a few more arriving. In the meantime, you can start coverage for the first script. See if you can finish in an hour and a half."

"Won't it take that long to read?"

She shrugs her shoulders. "Don't read the whole thing then."

Two hours later another recruit arrives. He looks my age, heavy set, with an overly optimistic attitude as if he were made to be taken advantage of. Helena sets him up at a computer across from me with his first script to read.

"Welcome," I say once she's gone.

"Hey, man. I'm Alec."

"Carson. How'd you end up here?"

"My girlfriend and I have been crashing at her mom's guest house. Time for us to get jobs."

"You know this isn't a job—I mean for money, right?"

"Yeah," he says amiably. "I'm hoping it will lead to one. As it was, I landed this through a connection."

An hour later an overly enthusiastic guy in his late twenties enters the room like he's grasped his chosen theme for the perfect frat party and cannot wait to share it with us. "Okay, guys!" He tosses a handful of comic books onto the conference table with a thud, spreads out a stack of covers featuring an elusive-looking female character who wears a bright yellow sash and holds what looks to be a knock-off lightsaber in her right hand. "What do you gentlemen know about comics?"

"Haven't read a lot of them," Alec says.

"Wrong answer!" the guy says.

I try to seem upbeat. "I've seen quite a few of the comic movies. They've been making them my entire life."

"That's better, man. What I want you to do is read some of these and tell me what you think. Like as a potential TV or film project."

"Do we have the rights to these already?"

"All in good time, friend," the guys says with a cryptic air to Alec's totally reasonable question. The guy spins in a half-circle before exiting, his loose tie fluttering like a feather.

"Who's that?" I ask.

"My girlfriend said there's someone at the company whose Dad is best friends with Mr. Eiley. He's just kind of here...but with a really nice office. Must be the guy."

We look across the way to see another sphere-shaped conference room like ours filled with *Iron Man* and *Avenger* posters on the walls. Overenthusiastic guy sits in a plush leather chair; he slips sleek headphones on his ears and begins to jam out. I stand for a stretch and take a peek at the rest of the production office, which by now has filled to its everyday capacity. Occupied assistants, half of whom are currently on the phone, jot down precise notes while wearing headsets primed to man an air traffic control tower. When they finish a call, they seldom look up.

The executives hold court in their tiny, well-upholstered offices, rarely making an appearance among the rest of the staff like vaulted sentinels, maintaining the required distance necessary to enact the deals, which generate the lifeblood of the place. When they do emerge, there's usually a problem, never one of their own making—even if it is. Sometimes they take a triumphant stroll to the bathroom, a noticeable bounce in their step. A deal may have been inked, but more likely, they've just finished those runny eggs I picked up. For the assistants, every snag is a potential obstacle to eventual advance-ment; they scamper from task to task like manic mice. When the assistants emerge from their partitions with good news, they're triumphant campaign managers armed with the winning electoral results. When they're caught in a muddle, low-grade anxiety gradually expands through the office, dispersed down to the interns. It spreads like a virus, primed to swallow everyone in its path on the way to irreparable damage.

"Doesn't it bother you that we're the ones reading these scripts?" I say conspiratorially when another hour's gone by and I'm halfway through the coverage on my second script.

"I like reading screenplays."

"No; I mean like, if we're not even getting paid, should we really be the first set of eyes on these scripts?"

"We had to do a lengthy interview for the position though."

"That's true," I say.

"Like I said, I don't know about you, but a connection landed me in the door."

"No, me too. I had a film school connection," I say.

Alec shakes his head. "You got to lay off the not getting paid thing, man. It's depressing me."

No additional interns arrive by lunch. Alec and I find ourselves in a cramped kitchen, which exudes a damp exhaust not unlike the break room of the movie theater Sebastian and I worked at in the Parish in high school. "Fix yourselves a plate of something from the fridge," Helena tells us when it's lunchtime without any other instruction except the note we should "absolutely not touch the hummus under any circumstances," as the hummus "belongs to Mr. Eiley." We find some bologna, some turkey meat, enough bread for one person, and some stale carrot sticks. A sizable portion of the fridge is filled with plastic containers of the aforementioned hummus. I stare at the tower of hummus a moment like it's the holy grail but venture no further. Alec and I sit back in our intern room. Catch a glimpse of the goings-on in the assistant section. Many are still on the phones: no designated lunchtime for this place.

"What do you want to do in the business?" Alec asks me between bites of his turkey.

"Write movies."

He looks puzzled.

"And television," I add. "I know they hardly make movies anymore. How about you?"

He points to the assistants through the glass window. "I guess what they do." He smiles, gesturing to the offices behind the assistants. "And then what they do."

"Nice."

"Isn't it kind of weird they have us reading scripts first?" he says. "You'd think they'd want us on the phones as a starting point."

I agree. "You gotta figure the scripts must be fairly low grade. We're the first line of defense, so most never need to reach the assistants' desks."

"A major assist to them, free of charge."

"You told me not to bring up the no pay thing."

"I know; I know!"

And then a screech of a scream rings out across the lobby, loud enough for us to hear through the glass. "Hey, everyone here needs to funnel back through the last three hours and tell me who the fuck ate my hummus?" Eiley's voice is a spinning Ferris wheel with no end in sight. "There are few rules in this office, but you all know the primary one, which is, of course, do not touch my damn hummus!" Alec and I rise from our chairs, our sodas in hand so it still looks like we're lunching while we acquire a better look. Eiley storms past the cubicles, leaving a trail of fetid angst in his wake. "You all think this is fucking tech? No one's breaking open the system here. You know how you succeed in Hollywood? Follow the rules. Especially my rules—regarding my damn hummus."

As far as rules go, only college students are allowed to hold internships, but somehow all the production companies skirted past that little rule. We sit down to finish our lunch, and my eyes wander over to Alec's plate; a medium-sized helping of a brownish, liquidy substance holds court next to the grapes he snagged: it's the hummus. He sees me looking at it.

"That's insane," I say.

He smirks. "Well, you got the turkey."

We're assigned individual delivery runs in the first few days; they take me to West Hollywood, Beverly Hills, and Silver Lake. This has to be the last industry in the country that still transports handwritten documents to people around town. It bothers me I'm driving my own vehicle. I do not expect the production company to have cars for our use, but the idea I'm sustaining my own risk in my own car running errands in heavy traffic without a paycheck is troubling. They say they'll reimburse me for mileage, the only check I'll receive. I learn to accept the traffic with greater ease and glide along like Han Solo floating away with the garbage in *The Empire Strikes Back*. On Friday of the first week, Alec and I receive a joint assignment: lunch. Helena hands us the order. "You two need to check every sandwich before you leave the deli. And I mean specifically open the sandwiches. Do you guys understand?"

"We do," I say.

"Don't bother coming back without checking all the sandwiches."

I want to ask her if she means we need to return to the deli if we forget to check, or if we're not supposed to return to the production company ever again if we fail to check the sandwiches, which begs the larger question: would we get to keep the sandwiches?

On the way to the deli in Santa Monica, Alec and I say little to each other. We drive down Wilshire with the windows open. I catch a whiff of the sandpaper air and start to feel claustrophobic inside my own car. I'm nervous about Helena's instructions regarding the order; she didn't take into consideration the logistics of inspecting thirty sandwiches. How am I supposed to notice whether there's mayonnaise or mustard between the meat and the bread without really getting in there?

We enter the deli, passing a serene scene. Young professionals relax and recline in puffy booths, leaning over hot corn beef and mustard sandwiches. We shuffle through an extensive hallway, a fast track to the kitchen. The waiting area's a miniscule corridor with whiffs of grilled deli meat mixed with our own sweat. I feel my body temperature climb as we wait for the completion of the sandwich order. Alec and I sit on narrow barstools, though it's more like I'm lingering in a hospital waiting room with the requisite level of uncertainty. I can smell the warm deli meat breaths of nearby patrons. Alec produces headphones. He listens to music on his phone rather than concern himself with watching for our impending order.

I nudge him. "Where are we going to check the sandwiches?"

"Who knows?"

A cook finally calls out our order in a growl. I walk to a narrow pick-up counter to find thirty individual wrappings, each snuggly stapled together in thin paper inside six larger plastic bags. It's as if the sandwiches are so tightly packed an intervention will be required to open them. "Is there a place I can check these?" I call out.

The cook makes a gruff sound. "What do you mean?"

"I need to check the sandwiches," I say pathetically, as if I'm speaking to no one.

He dismisses me with a wave of his hand.

I carry the six bags over to the barstools Alec and I were sitting on and open the first bag. Rip the first sandwich wrapping open; a rogue staple dangles, dragging bits of paper along with it as I continue to pull. The wrapping is intricate. Unwind and unloop the thing, hoping there's some way to put it all back together, although right now, I need to see whether there's mayonnaise inside this sandwich—damn the cost. The rye bread stares back at me, ready to admonish my inability to keep my hands from rubbing up against its elastic crust. Impossible to even see if there's really mayonnaise in there without maneuvering the two slices with my fingers.

Alec addresses me like he's visiting me in a mental ward. "What are you doing?"

"Trying to do my job," I say, fighting the sizable lump in my throat.

"Put it back in the wrapping," he says. "This place is way too packed."

I neglect to notice the clumps of additional people crowding around us, impatiently waiting on their orders. I regard the shredded sandwich with defeat. Once I look at the six bags holding the rest of the sandwiches, I wistfully realize my task is impossible.

We drive north toward the production company in silence. Alec shouldn't be embarrassed for my attempt to follow Helena's specific directions, but I know he is.

"How ya doing?" he finally says.

"Great."

"We'll tell her we checked the sandwiches," he says with a vacant conspiratorial air.

"I'm not going to lie to her."

"What are you going to say?"

"What are *you* going to say?" I pull up at the stoplight on 26th Street.

"We could say I thought it was a crazy request, but you tried. And it's still a crazy request."

"Might be a good time to remind myself we're not getting paid." We both laugh. Then I lurch forward, the seat belt catching me hard in the gut. It feels as if a rock has bashed into the driver's side.

Alec coughs from his parallel position, jolted forward against his seat belt.

"Looks like someone rear-ended us," he says.

The next hour finds my car getting towed to the Volkswagen dealership. Luckily Alec and I do not require medical attention, and we receive a ride back to the production company, where we triumphantly deliver the deli sandwiches absence any fanfare. Helena takes the bags and says nothing about checking the sandwiches. Right after lunch, Helena gestures for me to follow her.

"You need to talk to our lawyer," she says in a colder voice than usual. She leads me to an office in a hidden hallway I didn't know existed.

A stout woman in her fifties with a cigarette voice squints as I sit down across from her. "We heard you got in an accident this morning," she says as if she's beginning an interrogation.

"Yeah, unfortunately." I shouldn't expect her to ask how I'm doing, but I can't help it.

"What happened?"

"We were rear-ended at the stoplight on 26th and Santa Monica Boulevard coming back with the lunch pickup."

"This was your car?"

"Right."

"Why were you at the stop light?" she asks with suspicion.

"Because there was a stoplight." I flash her a confused smile. "It was red."

She makes a note on her legal pad. "Is there damage to your car?"

"They said I'll probably need a new bumper and tail light."

"Their insurance will cover it?"

"I hope so."

"This is the first time anyone's been in an accident at this company."

"I suppose when you send interns driving all over town all day long, it's bound to happen." My tone sounds too aggressive. "Our car was stopped at the light. It was completely the other person's fault," I add in a softer tone.

She makes another note. "Okay then," she says as if she's come across an interesting discovery. I harken back to when I was younger in the Parish. There was attention hoisted on me for some whispered ability. Now this ability is only a leftover crimson leaf lying in a thicket of snow; the office begins to close in on me. "Thank you," she finally says. "You can go back to work." The work I receive no compensation for. Shouldn't let the lawyer's vague disappointment affect me. This disappointment is key to wielding power in the industry. Place people in positions lower than they should be with minimal mobility, then act surprised when natural events occur, which are intertwined with a simple probability like a rear-ended vehicle—an unsurprising occurrence when you send car after car, day after day, onto the chaotic streets of West LA and the surrounding vicinity.

In the next week, I'm sent on fewer and fewer errands and sit mostly in the intern room by myself, reading script coverage. They place Alec on the phones. It's evident they're grooming him to become an assistant whereas it's clear the scripts are a dead end, even though the role utilizes my expertise. I reassure myself I'm here to obtain a writing connection, but this possibility appears unlikely.

A week later the production company holds a social gathering at a no-frills wine bar near the promenade. I decide the get-together will be my make-or-break evening. If I'm going to make connections with some of the executives, tonight's my chance. Alec tells me he'll be there, but after standing at the bustling bar amidst the frantic and intoxicated intern alumni for nearly an hour while I nurse a Coke because I want to remain sharp, he's still nowhere in sight. I position my body toward conversations, which seem perpetually in progress; my ability to join these convos with a witty remark or an insightful comparison remains elusive. I suspect I'm not as awkward as I feel on the outside, but sounds of constrained silent agreements amplify a cliquish atmosphere. Catherine Devine, the youngest executive at the production company and not far from my own age, sips from her wine glass during a lull between conversations, alone at a slim pull-out table. I swallow, then approach, opting to hold my drink instead of placing it on her table; don't want to appear like I'm colonizing anything.

"How often do you guys have these parties?" I ask.

She speaks to the side of my head as if direct eye contact will encourage me. "Probably not enough, I imagine. Once every two months maybe."

"This is my first Hollywood party," I blurt out.

She regards me with skepticism. She flips her head to see the rest of the room, her hair flopping toward me. She might be trying to get someone's attention to come rescue her. Then I think: rescue her from what? What if I really become famous someday? Shouldn't she be on the lookout for that sort of thing? Isn't that part of her job? I tell her my school and that I hold a B.F.A. in screen-writing. She says nothing. I consider enlightening her about my actor friend who's now on TV and who also starred in my plays, but I decide against it. "How did you become an executive?" I ask.

"An internship," she mutters.

"Did you become an assistant after that?"

She nods. She doesn't seem to enjoy socializing with the other executives or assistants. They're likely all rivals, conniving against each other for a finite piece of the pie, which Mr. Eiley sits on while he dips his whole grain organic crackers into his sizable hummus. She may see me as a rival as well, though I doubt it. Her charcoal gaze reveals her disappointment over speaking with an intern. My lower position precludes the conversation from venturing further. I surmise we're roughly the same age. I enrolled in film school; perhaps she got herself to LA even sooner. Now our roles circle each other like agitated fireflies in the night. She shifts her head again, pasting on a practiced smile—signals her exit. I know she doesn't want to look like she's flirting with the interns, but the way she insulates herself suggests something else. She remembers she was in my position; it quietly repulses her. She knows there are so few paths out of it. The competition—formidable—because the system resolves to reward not on merit, but on personality and attraction, at least until a certain climb upward is reached. True mentoring poses substantial risks. The mentee could rise up and surpass the mentor in record time. Best to keep a low profile. Best to cease curiosity until perhaps it's safe to do so, until one has risen to the height where it's comfortable, at which point it will become nearly impossible not to take advantage. Catherine floats away along with the stalled conversation to the table next to us, leaving me alone in the soft light. Maybe no one wishes to engage after my car was rear-ended. I quit the next morning.

West Los Angeles is all office parks and shiny, high-end gyms. Everyone's purpose seems fixed in this town unless you're in your car where I find myself with no set destination. I chose to follow my colleagues from film school, and while I'm thankful for the fact some of them are back at the house we share, I know I'm also more alone when I wake in the morning than I've ever been in my life. Something else lies just out of reach; a clarity I'm afraid I'll never grasp. I need to be pumped into "the system" as soon as possible; the thought of returning to our home in the Parish, empty-handed, with Sebastian still living there, makes my side ache, a continual sharp pain. It reverberates every time I consider no one cares about me here.

My film school friends, except for one, are employed, but not inside "the system." Louie teaches SAT prep on UCLA's campus. Oscar gets by from freelance web design. Devin, who does work within "the system," runs errands for a VP of a studio with the hopes that someday soon, the VP will recognize how efficiently he picked up dry cleaning as well as take into account Devin's B.F.A. from our university, which does sound impressive when you say it out loud. The three of them graduated the year before me, and while I'm thankful they secured a great place to live, I cannot believe they haven't found better jobs considering the education we received—and that's my problem: my high expectations coupled with the unforgiving reality facing us all.

With the car windows open, it's evident the air is crisper upon arrival in Beverly Hills. I pull into a parking structure with four floors. It's my go-to place for walking around and food pick-up. This afternoon I must pick up a job. With the air conditioning running, I scan through internships and assistant jobs, anything that's within walking distance from the parking structure. At this point, I care less about future career implications than an open position. I need something.

The reoccurring pain in my side returns. Then I see it on my phone—a welcome link to a website highlighted in blue: *Tunnel Vision Pictures*. Perhaps promising, especially as it's a block and a half away. The position looks like it *could* be paid, a producing role. I should be wary of the lack of specificity in the language. Instead, I welcome the chance that money could be part of the potential experience. Producing skills will be critical in the near future. Pat my pocket. If the Lexapro inside the case had eyes, they would be glaring at me. Think I'm finally ready to try the anxiety medication prescribed six months earlier. I was warned to take it on a full stomach. All I have is a smooshed Kind Bar hiding inside the glove compartment. I rip open the wrapper and begin to chew. As the globs of caramel stick to my teeth, my anticipation increases; I'm either about to feel calmer, drugged, or both. I loosen the cap to my thermos and drink. Swallow the tiny white pill.

I descend the stairs of the parking structure, my pace picking up. If I don't reach the offices soon, I may change my mind. The job description for the opening is vague at best, secretive at worst: it involves helping scout locations and securing further funding for multiple projects. I'm heartened at the word "further." Father did hand me money. My expectations are high.

On Beverly Drive, I ignore the angry panhandler outside the noodle place and keep my head aimed toward the intersection ahead where statuesque women with expensive gold strapped handbags stretch, waiting for the light to change. Red blurs into green. Dizzy but loose. Can feel it in my shoulders. A spark that settles through my stomach, my midsection, and down to my toes. I'm drunk at two in the afternoon with no alcohol in my system. Why did I take the first pill in the middle of the day? I grin at a dark brunette by the stoplight. Then again, why didn't I take this earlier? Breathe then glance at the woman again as everyone walks toward Wilshire. I feel like I've just written ten pages; warm, soothing feelings of accomplishment wash over me. I anticipate the interview. "I have no appointment," as Biff Loman would say, but I will show my proud face regardless.

An empty lobby greets me on the bottom floor of a mid-20th century apartment building—nothing but white paint and a lone end table next to an antique elevator that looks more like a dumbwaiter. Inside the elevator, I press the chipped button to the third floor, which points to a makeshift paper sticker of a dolphin eating what looks to be a film script. Evocative, yet pretty stupid. I stagger back, grabbing the wall. Focus on the blurry numbers on the elevator panel. They can help me regain focus. Take a breath and assess my current level of calmness. Not bad—only a little woozy. *I will make this work,* I tell myself as the door creaks open to reveal an empty loft space with no one around. My instinct tells me this is all wrong, but instead I take a handful of steps forward in order to temper the temptation to turn back.

"Come in already; I'm in the next room," a voice with an aristocratic South African accent pronounces. "We'll chat in a minute, mmh?"

I follow his directions, and in another moment I view a long black desk and, seated behind it, a fellow roughly my own age, perhaps even younger, trim and proper-looking in a tucked-in blue stripped button-down and dark jeans. He continues to type away at a laptop despite my intrusion into his world. His shoulders: arched and purposeful at the computer like he's preparing action plans for some unknown government. He waves his hand for me to move toward him with a certainty suggesting he knew I'd be arriving at this exact moment even though the meeting is impromptu and an act of desperation on my part. I've never heard of this production company until I read the ad earlier. Wouldn't be surprised if the ad already disappeared from the website I scouted, vanishing into the ether because everything in front of me is some hazy and desperate fever dream I've concocted from the Lexapro.

I walk toward the desk; the guy's not as trim as I thought. He's toned for some vaguely international sport like rugby. As I take my seat, I consider the odds he'll abandon the meeting altogether for a swim instead—if the meeting is real in the first place.

"It's not much, is it? Perhaps I'll purchase a couch for a waiting area when I have a spare moment."

"It's a lot of space," I say. "It's just you here?"

"Mmmh, for now. Tell me about yourself." His South African accent is some combination of British and Dutch that trips off the tongue like a memory at sea. With no film posters on the walls, this could be a job interview for anything. He gazes at me with a certitude I find alarming. How on earth is this guy in his mid- to late-twenties?

"I'm from Orleans Parish. I have a B.F.A. in Screenwriting." I tell him the name of my school, placing my resume on the table.

He flashes me a polite smile, unfazed as if in the land he hails from education doesn't matter—only family connections.

"I plan to write for television, but I also want to learn the ropes of producing," I say. He watches with simultaneous interest and skepticism. In a way, I've failed before I've begun. The people who succeed here begin by creating the impression they've already accomplished the things they wish to do. Maybe they start with an internship, but they learn the ropes and work for free in LA during the summers, when it's too early to hold an actual job. When they obtain their first position, they leverage it to the maximum degree, shuffling business cards across the table like they are Walt Disney's personal assistant.

"Yah, we don't have any television here." We both take in the empty room; the haphazard white paint left blotches in the corners.

"What does your production company focus on?" I ask.

"Film, my friend. There's nothing else. It still matters in this town despite what people tell you. I've got some ideas I've been churning around for a while now—I would welcome a writing partner."

The ad was vague as to whether the position was an internship or a job, yet it's quickly becoming neither. Does he plan on announcing his name?

"I'm Carson Levinson, by the way," I say.

He leans over the desk for a handshake. "James Paolan." He raises his nose like he smells something funky. "Is that a Jewish name?"

"What, Levinson?"

"Mmmh."

"Probably. I mean, yes. *I'm* Jewish." I'm a little flabbergasted at the remark, not because I haven't experienced anything like this before but because I *have*. Wouldn't have expected to hear such a comment in Los Angeles, land of sophistication and sizable Jewish population. "Is that okay?" I ask.

"What?" he says.

"That I'm Jewish."

"Yah, sure. I won't give you any shit over it."—as if I deserve "shit" for my identity and he's a generous guy for not dispensing it.

"I'm still not sure what your position is for," I say.

"It's a work in progress."

The barren walls of the sprawling workspace mock me from afar; I debate whether to simply leave. The lone sound of the air conditioning churns away. The ventilation reeks of risk and my own indecision. I consider thanking him and heading for the elevator, but I know there's nowhere else to go for the afternoon. Louie and Oscar will be home soon, aimlessly cruising Netflix or smoking up. Louie's accepted fewer SAT prep gigs lately, content to spend more and more time gaming online in the comfort of the house, which has begun to smell like marijuana and mold. I glimpse Paolan, and he smiles. There may still be a position swaying in the ether.

"What projects is the company working on?" *If this is a real company*, I think to myself.

"Two projects in the pipeline, my friend. Very excited about opportunities for growth." He crosses his arms as if the following were a speech he'd given more than once. "The first project is a space adventure. With the resurgence of *Star Wars,* I think there's opportunity to capitalize on this trend. I need someone to help me produce it."

"Is it *a lot* like *Star Wars*?"

"More like *Old School*—but in space. I also want to capitalize on buddy comedies."

His use of the word "capitalize" when talking about film concerns me. Also, buddy comedies have been popular for almost fifty years, so his film knowledge concerns me as well. Nevertheless, his confidence reassures, like if he continued to speak on a loop, the city would somehow fall into place and make him money without having to leave his chair. "And the other project?" I ask.

"The other project's mine."

"A movie?"

"Mmmh."

"What's the status?"

He rubs his temple. "Up here."

I'm now closer to walking out than when I arrived. How can this guy afford this infrastructure? "Why is it up there?" I ask, with every effort to make a personal connection instead of a critique.

He doesn't flinch. "No time to flesh it out. Not with everything I'm producing. You're probably wondering what it's about?"

"Bet it's special." I must want this job to throw unearned praise.

"It's about a secret society."

The dryness of my mouth takes over; his appearance blurs a little. "Oh, yeah?"

"A few families hold powers—magical powers. Passed down over centuries. Haven't worked out the details yet."

"What if the families guard a city?" I venture. "Like the power comes from the city's essence?" I glance down at the ground. Something's transpiring in this moment to make me feel powerless to the events unfolding in front of me. To this day, I still suspect my own mother possesses some kind of unworldly power. The secrecy she shrouded herself in when Sebastian and I were in high school only amplified my suspicions. Could this South African really know my family? Then I remember I added the additional detail about the city's essence on my own.

"I like that," he says.

"I could help you write it," I find myself saying.

"You should."

"I know I could write that story. You could show me what you have so far, but I could really create the world." I smile. "I know that world." Because I'm from there, of course.

"I gave you what I have so far."

"Well, I could definitely write this," I say. My confidence soars because someone has asked me to write something instead of quietly gauging my ability to answer a phone or fulfill an executive's complex wishes.

"If you were able to complete a full screenplay, I would be able to shop it around with my connections," he says.

What at once sounded like a job now reads as freelance. "Aren't you interviewing people for the producing job?"

"This is separate from that."

"And how am I doing on the job front?"

"I see no reason why you couldn't do both." His language is promising but vague. He adjusts his shoulders and neck; perhaps I should be concerned over his underlying strength. "I do see us working together," he finally says. His reply fails to clarify if money is involved. This must be what it's like for everyone starting out—money's an afterthought.

"I don't have a salary to offer you," he finally says.

Since this guy advertised a job, I've already caught

him in his first lie. Flinch at the idea my chosen major might be a loss, and perhaps I'm about to lose more. Even if I write an amazing TV pilot or screenplay on my own, which I know I'm fully capable of doing, no one's going to know me, and every gatekeeper's going to talk like this guy.

My thoughts accelerate to a time and place I've never seen; part of me's still in the room. My eyes drift toward the window as the walls stretch and bend like a *Chutes and Ladders* slide. The sun from the window glares back at me, and when my gaze returns to Paolan, something's irreparably different. I comprehend something else besides a person in front of me—brilliant hues of orange and pink reflect off Paolan's forehead. It's something intangible—an indiscernible energy on another wavelength from conscious thought—something I'm not supposed to have access to, but improbably do, right here in this moment, and it's telling me Paolan is a rotten person. I can somehow sense his quiet rage, his longing to hurl something toward unsuspecting bystanders.

"It's a good opportunity for your CV," he suggests. "You can write in Director of Development."

"Is that my position?"

He nods. "But no pay."

"Is there anyone else who works for the company? Really works for the company," I clarify.

"We have a CEO. He lives in Prague. And me. And a few others." He rises from his seat. Turns away and heads toward the window, as if I were not there. I follow him. The ivory-colored commercial buildings of Beverly Hills and the film and TV signs of West Hollywood come into view.

He gestures at one particularly large sign for a major film about to open, a tacit acknowledgment that I'm standing next to him. "You know what that sign represents?"

The director of the film on the sign is one of my favorites. Since fewer and fewer movies are director-driven, I assume the kind of film we're looking at, a true auteur film, is what the sign represents. I mention the director's name and the prestige classification of the film.

Paolan shakes his head. "Money. This film represents crazy amounts of money some guy is going to make on Friday. I can give you a percentage of both projects if you stay to help me. It's how I'm getting paid as well."

Father did give me money. I'm running out. I feel my stomach. Skipped lunch earlier and the day before that. I glance at my watch. Louie and Oscar are definitely playing video games by now. "Looking forward to helping you with both films," I say.

"Yah, that's good. You're making the right decision."

The lack of substance to Paolan's film idea should trouble me. It doesn't because it's such a good premise—not to mention the eeriness of my own childhood that I will add to the concept. I end up conjuring the world and the characters from scratch, drawing on some of my own suspicions of Father and Mother from back home. I personify a forward trajectory I've lacked since film school. I push an outline across the table to him at a café one morning with a request I'm not sure he'll accept.

"I'm going to end up writing most of this from scratch. I fully acknowledge you pitched the beginning of the idea, but since I'm creating this world, creating conflict and characters from the ground up, the work should belong to me if I'm to write this whole thing." Paolan's begun to pay me small sums for script coverage I write, the job portion of our relationship, but since the payments are pittance overall, I figure standing up for this point of possible contention is the least I can do for myself.

His eyes register amusement, but his facial expression remains unchanged. "Whatever you need to do to protect yourself," he says. Protect myself from him, no doubt. His answer signals no legitimate response, not for any kind of true partnership. However, since the writing is going so well, if he holds half of the connections he hints at, the risk will be worth it. I feel the pulsation in my head again, but I manage to shut it down. I'm terrified to access it.

A full evening of working on a screenplay—my own, not Paolan's—causes me to nod off in a tranquil respite. I tell myself even if I don't completely fall asleep, some of the script's issues will work themselves out, so I indulge in the haze even though it's only 9:30. My cell buzzes; arms flail to reach for it. Paolan's name flashes across the screen. I recoil, thinking he somehow knows I haven't been working on his project, and even though he hasn't paid me anything, he will somehow reach through the phone and grab my throat. Instead, Paolan communicates an opportunity: I'm to drive to the Palisades for a screening of one of the production company's films at the CEO's house. I thought the CEO lived in Prague.

The hills on either side of the car turn into modest

mountains as the car sinks forward, leaving Santa Monica behind. Hard to believe a turn in the wrong direction would send me hurdling down the mountain toward a fiery and premature death. That the car would explode upon impact with the rocks below is a given. I continue on Sunset, past the town square, and elevate skyward, gripping the steering wheel as I propel myself to a higher landscape than I knew existed. A helicopter is bound to be the only way this house could be reached besides the road I've taken—an unsettling thought.

At roughly 10:30, I arrive at the mansion, and that's what it is: an imposing gray brick monstrosity with a six-car garage and, go figure, a helipad. Paolan greets me at the door with the upbeat tone of a proud host, even though it's not his house.

"Glad you could make it, friend," he says. "Take off your shoes—then I'll introduce you to some people."

I certainly didn't need to be told to take my shoes off once I saw the pristine white floors with the multiple mats holding an array of footwear. The first thing that catches my eye is a long dining room table made of dark mahogany that looks more like it belongs in a boardroom. Electronic manila white shades appear to encase the dining room where the table is. Paolan leads us past a long purple leather couch on the way to the screening room. I'm relieved to see the film has not begun once we're inside; there's still time to meet people. A table of high-end vegan snacks is set up. I snatch a tiny bag of chickpeas before Paolan has a chance to introduce me to anyone.

Women in low-cut dresses mingle with overweight middle-aged men with thick, dark beards. Many of the men speaking with the women seem at least fifteen years older than the ladies. Is this really a company party? The energy in the room is vaguely sexual. If there was professional protocol for a workplace screening party, you'd only be able to find it in some book in the host's library I saw on the way in that no one's glimpsed in twenty years. My eyes search for the top row where I expect to find the owner of the mansion, but there's too much flaunting to hone in on a singular figure. Paolan shakes his head in annoyance when he sees me grab another tiny bag of chickpeas. "We'll get you a drink as soon as things settle down." He gestures at the man standing to my right. "This is Michael. He's our director of marketing."

Is Michael getting paid? I wonder. He's a short man who overcompensates for his height by sticking his chin out, which causes his gut to flail; he grips my hand in an unnecessarily tight shake. "Welcome to the party," he says. His accent is vaguely Eastern European and an octave lower than I expected.

"Did you work on this movie?" I ask him.

He gestures at the considerable number of people crammed in the screening room. "We all did." He gauges my reaction in the vicinity of doubtful and follows with, "I'm kidding; I don't know half the people here. Quite the get-together, huh?"

"Pretty standard for Demetri," Paolan says dismissively. Paolan leads me to a seat near the aisle in the first row. Paolan's definitely a bit on edge, like a woodpecker unable to decide which direction to face. It's the first time I've seen him unsure of himself—it won't last. In a meticulous way, he scopes out the room, deciding who to speak with next. It's clear Paolan lied about the production company functioning as a practically one-man operation. There's zero time to process the implications of his lie since he still holds all the cards.

On the bright side, I always wanted to attend a party like this. A woman in her early thirties with bright red hair sits behind us. Her hands grasp the back of my chair. "Who's this?" she asks Paolan in an upper-class English accent.

"Carson—meet Natalie."

"Hi," I say.

She grins then delivers a quick kiss to Paolan's cheek.

"Do you work for the company?" I ask.

"No way. Few of us actually *work* for the company."

I nod, my mind unchanged that Paolan's a liar.

Paolan rises and marches up the steps without a gesture in my direction, disappearing among the throng of people who are laughing and drinking while waiting for the film to begin.

Natalie regards me, no doubt measuring if I'm worth talking to while Paolan's away.

"Have you seen the film?" I ask.

"It's shit," she says. "Violent and repetitive. An overall lack of character development." She eyes me suspiciously, then in an upbeat manner says, "Paolan claims you write amazing coverage."

"Thanks. I'm glad he's said it to someone because he hasn't said anything to me." I've now delivered back-handed criticism, and I immediately regret it.

"He thinks highly of you. We were out the other night, and he mentioned how lucky he is you decided to work for him."

I hope my forehead isn't turning red because when Natalie uses the word "work," I experience a rush of misplaced rage; it's there just underneath the surface, waiting to tackle its prey at any number of inopportune moments. She probably thinks he's paying me way more than the fifty dollars a script he promised to begin paying me as soon as the new year begins. I imagine everyone in the room has money except me, but then the unease subsides when I speculate many in this place received money from their parents or trust funds, and perhaps that's what's sustaining them.

Natalie lowers her voice. "What do you think of him?"

"He's a smart guy."

"That's not a ringing endorsement. Just saying."

"What are you *just saying*?"

"Saying you kind of answered my question by not directly answering." Natalie glances to see who's standing near her. "He's unpredictable."

I turn to check, then lower my voice. "Paolan?"

She nods.

"Most people are unpredictable."

"You should be careful."

"What's your relation to him?"

She looks at me like a child she's only noticing for the first time. "I was his girlfriend. Briefly. There are far less resources in this town than there used to be. Gulfs of opportunity materialize; James fills in some of the gaps."

We both see Paolan descend the screening room steps, returning to hold court. "Suppose I should watch out for this Demetri person too," I say.

"That goes without saying," Natalie says.

The crowd at the top of the aisle disperses, and I can make out who everyone is talking to: a leering man with a fading hairline and tinfoil smile. He claps his hands, and somehow the room abruptly halts their conversations. "Movie time! Hope you enjoy our latest feature," the heavyset man says. "The acting isn't too hot and neither are the special effects, but I like the script, so there's lots to build on." I note this doesn't line up since the movie's already complete. Demetri continues. "Let me also personally thank James Paolan for his continued efforts behind the scenes to make it all happen, hah."

Paolan aggressively jostles my bicep, acknowledging my contribution to whatever the big guy just said even though I had nothing to do with this film. Now that the room is seated and right before the lights go dark, I can see many of the men sitting near the CEO are packing heat underneath their sportscoats, their handguns overtly protruding along their pressed sleeves. I gaze up at the opening credits, struggling to shake off residual paranoia.

About twenty minutes into the film, I decide the picture is one of the worst I've ever seen, which is a considerable achievement. I've seen an exorbitant number of films over the course of my young life. The critiques Natalie made a half-hour earlier are spot on: the movie is repetitive and does carry an overall lack of character development, but there's something else dangling just out of view. It's almost purposely bad—its awareness of itself is over-the-top and troubling, almost as if a decision were made to guarantee the film never receives a theatrical release. Why would a producer do that? My eyes again drift toward Demetri's bodyguards, the silver glint of their firearms sparkling in the light of the film projection. When a film receives a theatrical release, some type of publicity is secured. Unless the producers do not want publicity. Unless they do not want the attention.

MOIRA

2016

MOTORS BUZZ, PROPELLERS churning against grime and bog water, pushing it away to make room for the fleeing. Smells of mold and diesel gasoline disrupt my nostrils, make them wiggle, stored unsavory scents unleashed from land on the cusp of disaster. I feel impending disorder as we cruise past Elysian Fields in a high-powered motorboat headed for the school where my babies are, trying to avert a manmade crisis, our crisis, singlehandedly crafted by this man, my man. Why? 'Cause he left them at the school, so he could survey a wall he knows will fall. So he can lecture me, coax me into thinking my boys are grown men. Like him. Grown man grips the wheel of the boat like a cocksure badger. I see him hiding his shame with that half grimace where his lip's all turned out, too dry for my liking. This is what happens when I leave things up to him: against my better judgment.

Vibration and a hum. Pull my cell phone out. Voicemail? Is it working? Negative—leftovers from yesterday. Hit the favorites. My delicate finger dangles across his name with certainty. Tinge of temporary relief as I see the "C," merged with a dial icon. Carson. Engage.

No connection: a glimpse of a conversation we've never had. The major one. The one where I almost tell him what I've wanted to for ages. My past—his future. The precautions he must take. His abilities will metastasize sooner than I wish for him. I long for the peace of my kitchen, over-easy eggs simmering on the stove—no impending disaster on the horizon. Sebastian likes the eggs a little overcooked. Feeling of family in the air. My poor baby Sebastian. Cannot worry myself over you nearly as much as I ought to. How to care for the one without the gift is always a mystery to me.

And to think they're in the dreary school with the too-narrow hallways, so narrow you'll break your nose if you're not careful. See the little lost and found board fastened to the wall outside the principal's office with the unforgiving hooks. Nothing stays on those hooks long. No true honor code in place to ensure the items return to their rightful owner. The time Carson comes home to tell me his Volkswagen key fob, slipped from his grip in the parking lot. "Tell them in the office, I say. Maybe they'll help you find it."

"It's already gone," he says.

"Gone how?"

"I can't keep checking the lost and found board every hour on the hour, Mom. Someone will find it; place it on the board. Someone else will take it. They always do."

So there's your honor system: a smug factory of "how do you do" and "interesting perspective" and "will have to respectfully disagree." Wasps abound; feel the buzz. Was grown man's idea to send them there. His idea to move so close to the levee, so close to the flood: the unknown. Lots of ideas, and sure, I've followed them.

He's got that cute knowing smile. His chin tilts up a bit to let you know he's thought things over. Other things he's still thinking on; he'll get back to you when he can. I used to lie awake in my old childhood bedroom with the *Wings* poster and soccer trophies—picturing his square chin, his quiet soul thinking on things yet to occur, dreaming of structures he'd someday conjure that'd stretch to the sky. Immune to the folly of reality. Exempt from the moratorium on levee construction by you know who.

Back to my man, who steers the boat through livid bog water, wondering what to express, caught over the fact he should have retrieved his twin sons earlier, well before the furious wind and sullen streams laid bare to the Parish. Can smell the pomegranate tea on his breath, each exhale an accusation, each thought an indirect regret. Figure now is as good a time as any while we're stuck in the boat with each other to have the conversation he evades everywhere else. "We need to make a decision about Carson," I say.

Grown man lobs a sardonic smile my way. He still doesn't want to hear it. Doesn't want to hear about the abilities the Parish affords those lucky ones in her own unexplained, mystical way. Doesn't care to be reminded that after nearly twenty years, his powers have dwindled while mine have shined. Carson's on track for the same gift—likely more. So my man does the only thing he can manage. Changes the subject.

"Hey, we should let The Society know our location," my man says. "Maybe there's other boats that can be brought in. We can't just take off with our own kids and leave the others there."

That's exactly what the other parents would do, but I don't say such a thing. "Thought you put a call in already," I say instead.

"No one answered," he says.

"Did you call Raymond?"

He blows out saliva just as the plumes from an oil refinery find their way to our personal atmosphere. "I don't want to call him."

"I can call him," I say quickly.

His attempts to change the discussion flop in his face, so he returns to the subject of his son, trying his hardest to shroud his jealousy in his own mock attention. "Carson wants to go to New York, doesn't he?"

"It's all he talks about. Have you noticed?"

My man grins. "Once or twice."

There's my Victor. "If he wants to major in screenwriting," I say, "he'll have to go to college in New York. There or LA."

"And if he stays..."

"You know what happens if he stays."

Victor wipes his mouth with his wrist. I can see Carrollton up ahead. He's about to ask the question that's been bugging him. It's something he should be proud of, but he wears his displeasure too overtly. "If Carson stays, do you think he'll become stronger?" Victor asks. "Than you I mean?"

"I do," I say.

He nods, half envisioning the prospect against his better judgment. "Is that what you want?"

"The Society will expect him to lead," I say. "You know he's not the only potential successor. It could get ugly."

"I'm aware of this," he says in a modulated tone. "Though Raymond isn't exactly looking to step away."

"We still need to plan," I remind him.

"Where do you think is best for Carson?"

"How can I answer that?"

"You're his mother."

"Foremost I want him to be happy," I say.

"He's awfully young to take on the responsibility of The Society in just five years' time," he says.

Yet I sense Victor wants Carson to lead someday. Victor won't come out and say this, of course. If Carson stays in the Parish past the age of twenty-two, his full abilities will likely take shape. Victor and I lean forward in the boat and contemplate our ongoing stalemate as we zip through the dark water. In a cascade of stillness that threatens to upend our nerves, we each come to the conclusion that we want Carson to lead. But Carson will have to want it, and he's far too young to face such a decision. Up ahead, the boys' school greets us with its tall steeple and flooded parking lot. It's become a moat right in the middle of Uptown. "Let him apply to NYU," Victor says.

Can't help but be relieved. I know the danger my Carson could face in a future Orleans Parish.

MOIRA

1995

ON A BREEZY April afternoon, a party Uptown is brought to my attention. Sit on the porch in my orange sundress; summer humidity sticking to my shoulders, wishing I had someplace to go. A perpetual itch keeps changing its position under the slim fabric. Father approaches me in the front yard, tells me about this party. Something is off about his description of the gathering. It is too grand, too old-fashioned. Formal yet ethereal. "They don't have parties like that anymore," I say. "Only the most exclusive Mardi Gras balls."

He tries to smile. "That's the right idea."

"How would I get into such a party?"

"Only if you're invited, which you are. You always would be, once you turned eighteen. It's tonight. 7 PM. Tchoupitoulas Street. Must not be late."

"Can Dawn go?" I ask. I'm not very independent.

He shakes his head. "Only you. It's tradition, Moira."

"What do you mean tradition?"

And so he tells me. Know he's holding back; his lips pucker ever so lightly, as if he is trying to taste his own greying stubble. "We are part of an ancient family before the city was the city, before it was part of the United

45

States. Your mother's father was part of it. So was my mother. That's how I met Mama—at a party like the one you're about to attend."

This downright regal tradition he speaks of surprises me since we aren't particularly wealthy. Never see my father wielding any sort of power: he is soft-spoken, a bit of a pussycat. Mother is the tough one.

"They're like village elders on a larger scale," he says. "They've done questionable things over the years in the name of influence and hegemony."

"Questionable?"

"Sometimes terrible."

My astonishment at this newfound heritage dwindles, slipping to concern. "You join them for any of these *questionable* things?"

He pauses a moment, a silent debate waging inside him. Perhaps he wonders if he's already said too much. "They've helped my medical practice. When I started out, they brought patients to me. When Dr. Mendleson opened up four blocks away..." Can see him delve into the memory even though he has no intention of sharing it.

"What?" I say, trying to urge him on.

"You know what happened to Mendleson." He stares at the floor, betraying his embarrassment. "The health code violations. I'm not proud of the help, you see. At the time, I needed it."

"I don't want to go."

"Your mother will be disappointed."

"She's always disappointed."

"Regardless you must go."

"Why?"

"She is quite sick, Moira."

If there is still a heartbeat underneath my skin, I can't feel it. Is like being rear-ended in the seconds afterward, not knowing where the collision came from nor how to proceed. He lets me linger in this fresh world that is as familiar to him as the mole on his chin.

"It's cancer."

"What?"

"We have only recently discovered it. I think she can beat it, but we need to maintain our advantages."

If I keep asking questions, won't have to process what he utters. "When did she plan on telling me?"

"They have access to new medications."

"Who's they?"

"The Society."

My eyes register his desperation. "Is that what they're called?" Of course my mother can't tell me any of this herself, level with her daughter about what she's going through, stress the urgency of this debut.

My father shifts his feet. He is holding onto more than he wishes to grapple with.

"I'll put on my better shoes," I say.

"Moira. You watch yourself there." I suppose he suspects it'll be kid gentlemen. Kid gentlemen presenting themselves as such in their tailored summer wool, their primped-up bow ties. Kid gentlemen trying to persuade me how special I am, how I belong on their arm as if I belong anywhere they control. All pretension 'til they can possess. Then I gather he is concerned about something else. I don't ask what.

As I ride the streetcar further Uptown, I resent my father's wishes, the entire story of this sour lineage, my new responsibility. I am my parents' only child, their sole heir, and now, their principal hope. What if I wish to leave the city? What if I don't want children? I imagine ocean gusts roaring through my long hair. Looking out at high rises of northern Miami viewing peaceful Bal Harbor. Visited a friend there—10th grade summer. Languid trees you could nestle against. Picture myself as an adult in the Florida sun, unwinding in a kinder, softer humidity than I'm used to. The freedom of a far-off future, which earlier in the morning seems cursory and unimportant, now feels essential, even though it begins to evaporate in the cool night air; it slips through oak trees casting covert nudges against my shoulder blades.

A high-pitched screech from the streetcar wheels mixes with the mild, slimmer heat, signaling my arrival at life's next stage. My mindset as I move away from the tracks to my intended address is to make an impression, make an effort for Mom. Catch an inkling there might be no turning back once I enter the ominous-looking bronze gate on Tchoupitoulas Street. Two reserved sparrow sculptures beckon me inside.

Black walls and forest green carpeting greet me upon entry. Framed paintings of men signing lengthy documents and surveying land in the 1700s adorn the walls. These men seem to take refuge in these walls: inside this building they still controlled things. They tease me with their self-satisfied smirks, their furrowed brows. I recognize the background of some of the paintings: an earlier Royal and Decatur Street in particular, an intimate serenity no longer present in the cobblestone streets. A lone painting features a young woman—she cradles a fussy newborn in her arms. Or course she does. A man, the likely father, stands off to the side, again surveying land, already uninterested in the daily toll of child-rearing: a regular Dimmesdale from *The Scarlet Letter*.

A tall Hispanic woman with deep sea eyes in a mauve dress strides toward me, her hands outstretched. A couple of lifetimes seem to dangle in front of me as she grips my wrist, yet her figure, skin, and shiny cheeks suggest my same age. "We've been expecting you," she beckons. "The ceremony's about to begin."

Ceremony? She leads me out of the spacious parlor and down a corridor that could have doubled as a secret tunnel in an earlier time. Who the tunnel may have deceived is anybody's guess. Little time to think about it because, after a handful of steps, we enter a crowded auditorium that feels too large to fit inside this structure. Several young couples eye me, some with open disdain, some with mild annoyance. A heightened curiosity emanates from a throng of single young men, rather boys, roughly my age, standing near the stage, away from the couples at the tables. The single boys wear dark suits with bright ties: royal blue and blood red as if they were child corporate lawyers. The men accompanying the women are clothed in lighter tones—no ties. I am ushered to a row of folding chairs in front of the stage. Other unaccompanied women sit there; they're roughly my age, though some are a bit older in their late twenties. The older ones eye me suspiciously. They arch their backs and stretch their necks, yearning for a sense of territorial control they seem to lack. In some of them I can sense seasoned sophistication rubbing up against panicked urgency. Since no single women in their thirties reside in this throng of damsels, time is not on these girls' side, not in the world of this gala. An older woman, my grandmother's age, ascends the stage, and without a word, sounds of chairs skid and adjust; no need for this woman to utter a sound to garner attention.

"What a pleasure to see you all tonight," she says. Her enunciated speech suggests her desire for control. Two young boys take their seats on either side of me without so much as a glance. I focus on the woman. What threat does she pose underneath her broad smile? Part of me wants to pique the interest of one of the boys despite my unease at the whole situation. I try to remind myself the safety of home is only ten minutes away. It achieves nothing.

"Welcome to the 389th annual Summer Soirée. I expect you brought your appetites and your dance shoes. In just a moment I will introduce our beloved Raymond. And I mean that. *Beloved.* But before I do, let me say I have cherished my time serving our cause these many years, years which have flown by when I think back on it, and I do enjoy thinking back on it. Some of you I will miss. Some of you less so, but know I will continue to hold all of you in my utmost regard." She takes a moment to gaze out at the audience. There is a finality to this slight speech. Her eyes take their time with each row, making mental notes of who has snubbed her. The woman maintains enough youth to still settle scores someday soon. When she is finished with her de-marcations, she walks backward as if the wind has already whisked her away.

The two boys next to me fidget in their seats as a tall middle-aged man struts down the stage. His gregarious swagger belies a silent menace. I wonder if anyone notices. He places his hands in his coat pockets, and, like the lady before him, takes his time glancing over the audience members, although this time reminiscing isn't the objective; he instead seems to scope out intruders. I'm one of them. Heart pounds. Throat tightens. Want to leave, but how can I with such sustained attention focused on a stage so close? He detaches a microphone from its stand. Whatever he intends to say must require an amplification the older woman found unnecessary or didn't have access to. He wets his lips and leans in. "It was exactly twenty-five years ago tonight I moved here from New England. I'm not afraid to admit it." A few laughs from the audience. "That's right, you southerners."

His voice travels the room like a combustible firecracker. "I graduated college in May and wanted to start my life where it began," he continues. "I knew little of my birthplace at the time nor of my birthright on my mother's side. I did not distinguish myself in high school, but in college, I found my footing. I was what they called 'a late bloomer.' Real estate was where my heart was. Cleaning up homes, making things presentable. Whatever needed fixing I was game. The buyers—they were my audience. Anyone who entered a home could be a potential buyer. That's how I approached them—each fellow deserved the full assault. And let's be frank. It was an assault." He lets the word hang in the air a moment. His expression changes; earnestness transitions to aggression. He leads with his shoulders now. Each phrase is a windup to some uncharted territory, a new idea with the potential to inspire or instill fear in his followers. "By chance I learned my family was, for generations, a part of our little coterie in this city. It was incumbent I discover the mystery surrounding my origins. It was essential I leave my life in New England and journey to this city, meet its people." Where is he going with this? I can't decide if the speech is about him or the organization. Probably a little of both. "There is a reason this city maintains a specific reputation," he says. "Its ability to conjure wonder is fundamental to its identity. How does this so-called wonder happen? Only one way. We do it. You. Me. *All* of us." He hisses with enthusiasm. "We do what needs to be done. Sometimes they try. God bless them. They really try. You know who I speak of. They cannot see what we see. They lack the vision we possess. You have it. You wouldn't be here if you didn't. So start using it. Soon it will be time for a new group to take the lead."

The boy to my right smiles.

"But not yet," Raymond corrects. "Not quite yet." The tension in his face releases. The preaching portion appears complete. "Grab yourselves a dance partner and get on with it, why don't you."

Both boys on either side of me turn my way, looking down at my shoes as if they are the official pathway to a dance. From their viewpoint, I shift from an afterthought to a necessity in a second flat. Need to run.

"Haven't seen you before," the tall one says.

"That's cause I've never been here. Not at all sure what here is."

"It's a club. There's little reason to think it's anything else," the shorter one says.

"You want to dance?" the tall one asks.

Find myself giving the tall one my hand. I have already been transported to an earlier patriarchal time; no reason not to double down on the protocols of dancing etiquette from a bygone area. He forces a grin as we reach the designated dance area. As I place my hands on his willing shoulders, it is hard not to think of my mother. Other girls may be excited by the prospects this room holds; I can't help but wonder how she expected me to go through with this on her behalf. Did she really presume I'd begin dating one of these kid gentlemen? Mom, a public defender, is downtown this evening working on a major case. No time to consult or complain to her before I leave. Or ask her why she hasn't told me she is sick.

"My family is one of the oldest in the city," the tall one says. "We've been here since the beginning. We make a point of making our presence known from time to time."

"What does that mean?" I say.

"My father is a city councilman. We also own Lyon Pharmacies."

"That's y'all?" I notice he uses "we" and "our" when speaking of his family—why wouldn't he? Because he didn't actually start the pharmacy or run for city councilman—that's why. "Are you here to meet someone?" I ask.

"It's why everyone's here."

And there it is: a rushed matchmaking outfit designed to find eligible young ladies for the boys—not the other way around. Yet isn't my mother part of this lineage as well?

The tall boy's eyes begin to look me over in more than a casual manner. His field of vision rests at the hem of my skirt. Not the hem. My left thigh. Already picturing what it'd be like to be alone with me.

"You going to college?" I ask.

"Vanderbilt."

"Is the plan to return afterwards?" What an odd thing to ask him.

He smiles noncommittally. "What about you?"

I press forward on his evasion, estimating this little club requires a robust post-college twenty-something population. "Is that the plan?"

"Yes," he says. "And you?"

"I'm staying here. UNO."

His voice hardens. "It's encouraged we leave the city. It's our only chance to."

My eyes wander toward the other boy who initially sat next to me. Does he manage to find a dance partner too? In fact, he does. A lanky blonde, taller than this boy. She attempts to keep her footwork in step, his coordination a loose wheel axle. She wants this and is willing to do whatever is necessary to keep in step; who knows what the boy might offer in the future? Yet why does she need any of "this"? And why do I? Glimpses of my mother clenched in future pain from her cancer flash in and out of my field of vision, my father's plea still the dominant voice of the evening.

"Are you okay?" my dance partner asks. His vacant eye sockets implore my attention.

"I'm fine." But I'm not. The gaze of an outsider springs from the dessert table. The man who demanded our interest earlier, Raymond, looks on in piqued curiosity as he samples a piece of watery key lime pie. He takes his time savoring the tart. I don't want to know why I attract his attention.

Meanwhile, my dance partner tries to project a

possible future between us. "I plan to return to the city for law school," he says. "After that, I will settle into my father's law practice." Never heard the choosing and beginning of a profession sound so luxurious, like "settling" into the perfect position on a beach towel. Will this guy really find life that smooth?

Raymond takes a last bite of his pie then marches in our direction. Should I flee? The door, a good fifty feet away, seems insurmountable with all the mazelike dance traffic.

Raymond arrives in the middle of a Phil Collins number, an aching melody that cries for emotional relief. He lets loose a murmur into my dance partner's ear. "Take a break, son." The swiftness at which my partner leaves without a goodbye is startling. Raymond flashes the grin of a concerned parental figure as if he were my father's golfing buddy saving me from some unwanted advance at a country club. "Might we dance," he says.

I awkwardly place my arms on his shoulders, shoulders far too old to softly rest one's hands on. I try to convince myself this gentleman vaguely knows my parents in an effort to keep him in that elder-parental zone. The idea of him as a suitor is not fathomable.

"Enjoying the party?" he asks.

"A little."

"We'll need to increase your level of enjoyment, I think." I don't like the sound of that. "This is your first time here is it not?"

"It is." I check to see if anyone is looking at us. As far as the other dance partners around me are concerned, our space seems off-limits for viewing.

"Your father told you little, did he?"

The saliva recedes in my mouth. "You know him?"

"Of course I know Oliver. I'm sorry to hear about your mother."

My hands drop to my side. Shaking my head in dismay, I search him for an explanation, though I don't really care to hear any. Who *is* my father? Or my mother for that matter? It is like I don't know either of them. And this man does. "Who told you she was sick?" I ask.

"Do not worry. It was only this afternoon I spoke with your father. Your face tells me you only recently found out. I imagine this is a difficult time for you."

"He told me before I left for *this*," I say, gesturing at the room. "Whatever this is."

"A collection of like minds. Nothing more. Nothing less."

"Seems a little more than that," I say.

"Your father wants the best for you. You shouldn't fight that."

"I'll decide what I want."

He moves in closer. "Of course you will," he says.

We lock eyes. Catch a whisk of his scent: peppermint and musk, his aggression oozing through all of it. He wants to touch me. Wants to show me what his little club is capable of. A drop of sweat from his forehead falls onto my dress. I ignore it. He doesn't bother to wipe his glossy face. He gestures for me to move in closer. Will not consider, even as I move nearer. His breath entangles me: potent. A little sweet, but lethal. I want to shove him but only for a second. I'm now incredibly nauseous. Losing my balance, my knees give way. No way out; I feel resigned. For a moment, I step out of myself, watching him watch me. I tumble forward.

And into new hands. Not Raymond's. The new hands cradle, then prop me up. The hands ease me back to a standing position. It's a young man: maybe still a boy but older than the others.

"You alright there?" he asks. Whatever Raymond has been doing, it is over. Raymond's attention shifts to the young man holding me up.

"Moira, this here is Victor Levinson." I never told Raymond my name. "Victor, why don't you dance with Moira awhile. I need to check on some guests." Raymond scuttles away, leaving me to figure out new meanings of the word "awhile."

"Thanks for your help," I say to the young man.

"Saw you dancing with him. Thought I'd keep an eye on you."

"Glad you did."

"I'm Victor."

"It seems that way."

"And you're Moira."

I just nod. He is half a foot taller than me, but it feels like more. His bushy eyebrows cast a perpetual arched glance. He cradles my waist with a care no one has ever taken.

"This is your first time here," he states like a fact.

"It's obvious, right? Still haven't figured all of it out."

"Not sure I will either," he says.

"Look at these people; I mean, how could you?" Most of the room is paired up—both young and old, a certain perfunctory calmness in their rhythms I find unsettling. The music changes to a 1940s number. A somber tune. A trumpet wails in the distance, depicting a mysterious love story gone terribly wrong. Victor leans in. I grip his shoulders tighter. As we move to the music, our rhythm arouses a restricted tranquility, a localized cocoon of protection amidst a hungry, calculating energy. He's different than everyone here. Perhaps weaker. Shouldn't his sensitivity be a strength? I think so, and yet I can imagine it isn't the essential ingredient required to thrive among this community.

His whisper toys with the air around my lips like a child blowing bubbles for the first time. "Raymond did something back there. Didn't he?" he asks.

I nod.

"Try not to talk to him again, if you can."

"Do you know him?"

"We all do. Some more than others. Everyone wants to understand him, despite our best judgment."

I make sure no one can hear what I say next. "This isn't just a club? Is it?"

He grins like a catty orca, seconds away from blowing water in my face. "What do you think it is?" he asks.

"More than a club," I venture.

"Some people have abilities. Abilities that allow them to take advantage."

I try to internalize what he says as I think back to my entry through the ballroom. "I can sense it," I say.

His lips crinkle. "Really."

Close my eyes. No one smokes, but the space does. The cool gusts of air conditioning merge with a musk that resembles heartbreak and fury, fizzing at the surface, ready to lure an unsuspecting person to its contrary will. I wish I could sort through the covert chaos, try it on and figure out how to maneuver its subtle manipulations. But then I lose hold of it, and Victor stands before me, almost relieved as if he can sense my inquisitive intrusions. "Or maybe I can't sense it," I say, purposely backtracking. "What's your ability?" Now I might be having fun for the first time this evening.

"I can see the future sometimes," he says.

"Only sometimes!"

He looks hurt. "I'm serious."

I study him. "I know."

"It's selective. What I'm able to see." His smile startles me when our eyes meet again. His lips pucker. He debates whether to reveal more.

"I believe you," I say.

"I know you do."

"Tell me something from the future then."

"I don't think so."

I touch his arm. "I insist."

He turns his head to make sure no one is in earshot. "In twenty-one years come July...a hurricane will nearly destroy the city." He looks down at the floor. "And our twin boys will be stranded at their school."

SEBASTIAN

2022

IN THE UNRELENTING doldrums of the coffee shop where colleagues, lovers, and lone individuals grapple with the unending trajectory of life chugging along, my date makes a calculated decision not to allow for a beginning bond between fellow young wanderers. Between these intakes of breath and pauses, her composure transitions—from possibility to certainty; from subtle yearning to flight. My date relays a scenario where she could not see a future, any future, between us. This change in the air occurs in a matter of seconds, and when it's complete, I wonder why we grabbed coffee in the first place. There was a chance somewhere—I swear—sandwiched between her cranberry muffin and my strawberry-banana mint smoothie with coconut milk. I didn't do anything to precipitate the chance, nothing to accelerate or quicken the pace of desire, and now I regret my actions or lack thereof. She's already gripping her purse and scooping some of her crumbs left from the muffin. I already regret the next time I'll say the exact same things, in the exact same coffee house, on a nearly identical date. I picture myself talking to the girls back in my high school, especially the night we waited for the storm to rip through. I wanted to be a hero. I thought if I somehow saved everyone, I'd be taken seriously. Carson took my idea to Wentworth, but the plan was dashed not long after it was conceived. Never knew what to say back then either.

My date nods. A polite turn of the head, a gesture of minimal regret, and she's already maneuvering, on the way out, squeezing between little green stools with bases too narrow to sit customers comfortably. I let the coconut milk from my smoothie linger on my taste buds as long as possible and search the room, maybe looking for someone feeling lower than me. No such luck at first. A young couple with a baby girl sits in the corner; they lounge on either side of her stroller, pushing it back and forth, a quiet secret between them. Two tables to my left sit a man and a woman, both dressed for business, a possible first date going much better than mine just did. His right hand is only centimeters from her hand; both are engaged in what appears to be meaningful conversation, so much so, they don't even realize there is legitimate tension between them, a natural ease of language and care pervading their table.

See this guy, three tables to my right. Stack of papers sit in front of him. Must be an English teacher. Two piles: one with his markings, one without. He reads each one with a rhythm that's private only to him, projecting proud optimism not unlike the kind Carson likes to throw around. Wears khakis and a pale blue button-down with a bright blue tie, but it's the shoes I can't take my eyes off of—light brown with a beige scroll-like pattern that traces around the edge of the front toe and back toward the heel. Taps his right foot against the concrete floor, as if his marking papers is intellectual and calming at the same time. Doubt it, but he seems to think so, all from the momentum in his wrist, which holds the pen with a grace and assurance I wish I could summon on my best day.

I enjoy reading. Like a fluid turn of phrase. Love to perform. I attempt to picture myself in a classroom. What would it look like? What would I teach them? What was I taught? Assume I'm watching a high school teacher while I sit in this coffee house. The guy's too young to be a college professor, and the papers appear too orderly and too long to be from middle school.

Already I can't wait to tell Carson. I'm picturing him working in an identical coffee shop in chaotic midtown Manhattan, his hands beginning to split from the cold. Works on one of his precious screenplays, considering which words to select that will imbue the character some director will conjure on film, even though we both know it's the actor who will determine the emotional tones. Audiences will decide if they like this character because of the performance—not because of how many nonsensical ellipses Carson decides to dribble in. Of course, Carson's no longer in New York—he's in LA.

Need to move into my own place. I know that. Why would a date want to go on a second one with someone who lives with his parents? Need to do better—stop lying to myself. Can do a better job of pursuing the truth. After all, that's what a teacher does: pursues the truth for the benefit of his students.

Home is not the same without Carson. Father emotes less than he did before, which wasn't much in the first place. He comes home late in the evenings; at that point

I'm usually reading a play, scoping out new monologues. He slides the kitchen door to a close. More comfortable for him to assume I'm asleep than to engage in mundane conversation, which carries the potential for dis-agreement—his disappointment in me occasionally erupts like a geyser. Fixes himself a sandwich, usually ham—sometimes bologna: a child's meal. Spreads the mustard like an orchestra conductor as if the act of sandwich preparation were the one thing he has total control of for his day. He used to work on a massive levee, but The Society shut it down. Takes his time with the sandwich, opting to warm the bread up first. Maybe that's why he shuts the kitchen door; doesn't want to wake me. Still think it's for fear of possible conversation. The man's had zero thoughts on my lack of employment or on my living at home. September will transition to October, and I doubt he'll notice. Lately I wonder why he doesn't come home for dinner, unless his purpose *is* to stay away.

Sometimes I catch Mom staring into the metallic microwave door, catching a glimpse of her reflection. She appears mostly the same as she did when Carson and I were in high school. Her face is fuller. It's obvious she's now dying her hair. Her height does a thorough job of obscuring her age; it always has. Day before she goes to the salon, you can see the quiet gray streaks sneaking through around her ears. Something's going on between them. Logic points to Mom's further involvement in The Society. She no longer bothers to hide it from Father. If there is a gulf between them, I'm making it deeper.

How I ended up at home is not entirely clear to me. Was keeping up with my reading as the end of last semester approached. Some of my other classmates secured internships in New York or Chicago, but those weren't jobs. However, I now see how the internships could lead to jobs in the future. An impending dread washes over me whenever I send an application out because I know the letter will result in rejection before I even press send. Ruminate whether to relay Father with my apprehensions, but I opt for independence, and independence is silence.

Believed I could save money living at home while working at my first job—once I found the first job—then I couldn't find the first job. It is difficult to find a job when you don't know what you want to do. If I taught, wouldn't have to be a teacher *forever*. Can see myself doing teaching in the classroom: engaging in leaderlyesque activities.

Later in the evening, in the comfort of my room, which has been my room for quite some time, skim the school websites in the area. The school year's already begun; what was I thinking? As if I could begin teaching due to the sole fact that I want to. Could try to secure something downtown—maybe I could intern at Father's architecture firm. Then again, Father wouldn't help me nor would he allow it. Yet what if a school offered an internship? Delay the inevitable while I search the web. Know exactly where such an internship might exist. The internship may even exist just for me. Why do the people we admire the least hold the keys to allow us to keep going?

Find myself sitting in a wooden-paneled office lined with lacrosse trophies along a wall space where more degrees should hang. A grayer, less jaunty George Wentworth sips tea from his mug with the embossed patrician-looking logo of my high school on it. His face wears a perpetual upper-class expression; the mouth is always open a sliver. He sizes me up like a man about to participate in a duel.

My resume sits in his hand as he combs down the employment column. He frowns. Not sure what he expects to find as I'm fresh out of college. That's his thing though—moderate surprise at his own displeasure over information he should expect. It's another way he gains ground on everyone he interacts with.

"What was your internship in college?" he asks.

"I worked at the Clam."

"Here in town?"

"In the summers in their literary department. I read and evaluated scripts."

"What about their education department?"

"Sure, they have a good one."

"Did you work there?"

I want to say, "If you think that's important, I'll go back in time and do it right now." Wouldn't be surprised if he agreed to such a proposal.

"I helped out with some of the presentations to visiting schools." This isn't true at all, though when it's out of my mouth, I realize the falsehood cannot be taken back. I pretend the event occurred as if the new memory will lodge itself squarely among real ones, preventing a future slippage of my true timeline. "It was a good experience," I add. I laugh a little at the sheer disingenuous tone I can't help but produce.

He brightens. "That's great, Sebastian." He addresses me by name for the first time today. Unbelievable. He loves my manufactured experience. "In a perfect world, what subject would you teach?"

"Acting. Then English. I was a Theatre major, but I took a handful of English classes." Wentworth's still thumbing over my resume. "Do you have any openings?" I ask.

"Sort of. We could use a long-term substitute teacher. We also need someone to help out with the clubs. Especially if students want to start a performance one."

"That would be great."

"Don't agree to something before you know the parameters, Sebastian. As an alumni, you should know that." He finally looks right at me. "This would be a good start to a teaching career. On the days you're not called in, you could shadow some of our teachers. I'll make you a list."

"Thank you."

"Haven't hired you yet. What can you offer us?"

"I'm a good theatre director."

"There's plenty of good directors in the city."

"Are there?"

"Plenty," he says with assurance. "What sets you apart? You've got to respond to a question like that."

"I know."

"So do it."

I appreciate his hard-nosed approach. Never got to see this side of him. Never got to see what went on in the wood-paneled, glass-windowed office. Sometimes I'd meander during a free block when I was a student, try to eavesdrop on what a particular parent's perceived grievance might be—usually grades.

"I know the school well."

"Sure."

"There was the time we all got stuck in the hurricane. I came up with this amazing plan to clear everyone out of the building. No one went for it."

For a moment Wentworth's demeanor changes. I can see him reconsidering his opinion of me.

"You mean *I* didn't go for it. Was a valiant effort; however, I explained to you at the time why it would not work. Your job right now, Sebastian, is to impress me. So do it already."

"I'm a proud alumnus."

"Go on."

"I bring a special kind of perspective. Kids like to see that."

"There you go."

"I think it would help the students to see a figure they could look up to. Especially a younger, more recent alumnus."

"Now you're talking. I was thinking the same thing. That's your angle, Sebastian. Everyone needs one, and that's yours." He grins; it's clear he's pleased with himself, and it looks as if I'll secure my first job by the time I leave this office. "That will be your role in the school. Talk up that alumni angle. Capitalize on your high school years here and how they helped you. Be a positive role model. Do you think you can do that?"

"Absolutely, sir."

"I know you will."

I pass students in the constricted hallway as I make

my way out of the administrative wing. They carry themselves with stiff postures, like sad giraffes, perhaps coming to grips with the truth they will soon have little control over their lives, and there's nothing they can do about it. Ascend the winding staircase to the third floor where students are busy scarfing their lunches. Wentworth wants me to meet the Fine Arts Chair. I stop before I reach the slew of tables. At each table sits eight students and one teacher, no different from when I was there. A woman in her forties spoons some coleslaw into her mouth, avoiding eye contact with the rest of the students, who are busy making plans, sharing secrets, and straining through some type of painful lunch conversation. Some teachers maintain a blank smile, partaking in casserole and vegan burgers with students during what should be their break time, the teachers struggling to convey the impression they're participating in the most natural scenario in the world. From the way some of the students gaze down at their plates with a distant hopelessness, one can tell they've already got a foot out the door of this place, even though they look to be only sophomores.

Another teacher in his late fifties regales his students with some kind of amusing tale from his past. I hear "France" and "Britain" mentioned between mouthfuls of pasta as he encourages them to "broaden your horizons." Am I going to be one of these teachers? Is this lunchroom my future?

Follow Wentworth as we head toward a table of teachers—I remember this now. On certain days, teachers are allowed to sit with each other instead of the students. Never gave it a thought back then, but I can feel their slow-moving relief emanating from their seats. How thankful these teachers are. We used to resent the teachers sitting with us anyway; why not let the teachers socialize on a regular basis? I approach the table, and as I do, it begins to sink in I'll be the youngest teacher here. I shake the Fine Arts Chair's hand. Everyone's going to like me. I know it.

The school auditorium hasn't changed: insufficient acoustics, dreary angles, a stage far too small for the size of the house surrounding it. I agree to advise the sketch comedy club already in existence. The students write their own skits, then direct and perform them for a school fundraiser. I was sketch captain when I was a student, but we never had an official club even though we met all year round—we were pretty awesome, though. Our best sketch captured my portrayal of Wentworth—never locked down his voice, but I nailed his walk, an upper-class shuffle designed to alert everyone in sight old wealth was on the march. I wore a pinstriped suit with a vest and a monocle. He didn't show up the night we presented the skit, which involved a weird scenario where Wentworth found himself alone at a public pool shortly after the hurricane, and no one else remained in the Parish.

There's fluidity at private schools that allow students to start clubs with minimal infrastructure or supervision. The fluidity creates a multitude of leadership positions for students regardless of the number of people in a given club—a helpful perk for the college application process when it comes time to describe the obscure idea of "leadership." At our school, students could hold the positions of president, vice president, and treasurer for a club of only five people. You need a teacher advisor to create a club, but as long as the advisor checks in once every few months, you're golden. I was vice president of the theater club when I was a student. We met four times. If you're a teacher, often any attempt to corral students to do anything more than eat snacks together will result in missed meetings, miscommunication, and pathetic entreaties by the teacher. Now that I'm a sub, my club presence would increase my faculty prestige, yet the kids will likely resent me being there in the same way I felt when I was here not long ago. So, I'll need to impress the kids quickly and decisively.

A club is dead on arrival if the teacher starts the club on his own. So along with student buy-in, you also need that initial effort on a student's part to fill out the paperwork, shepherd the thing to its first meeting. Wentworth helps me in this regard; on my first day, he introduces me to the school and notes my previous improvisational background from college. I treat the first Intro to Acting class I sub for like a performance on its own. In the circular black box theater—the same theater where I played Don Quixote in *Man of La Mancha*, which I do not shy away from bringing up in the first two minutes—a student asks me to elaborate on my experience. I use the occasion to advertise the positive attributes one could garner by practicing improvisational skills and how "I hoped a student might start a club." Declan Sullivan, a wily sophomore with dreams of starring on Broadway, approaches me after class.

"So you'll advise an improv club if I fill out the paperwork?" he asks. I notice how the kid employs an odd conditional statement to make a request. "I've been waiting to start a club like this for a while," he says.

I put my signature down and note how much better this already is than sitting in a coffee shop daydreaming about some potential job in the hypothetical future. Now I'll help with two clubs—already on a roll. I proceed toward the administrative wing, looking ahead as if an indiscriminate phantom lurks just ahead of my steps. My new determined nature looks good on me. It will be easier to look up to someone like me than a graying fifty-year-old man. Two male students, both with an athlete's posture and probably juniors who look older than me, eye me curiously as I arrive at the administrative office. Juniors are most suspicious of new arrivals. They still have enough time at the school to care what's inside it, yet most of them are already set in their ways. The one on the right dips his left shoulder ever so slightly so that the side of his bicep plugs me in the arm. A fast panic overwhelms my equilibrium. Do I engage them? Ask them their names to record some impending punishment, which the Vice Principal will probably ignore? Can't recall many detentions distributed when I was a student.

I should decide this instant, and if I do nothing, these kids may enact something far more treacherous at a later date. Stop short of the door, spin my back to the wall to survey the scene, but the two guys are gone. I decide I do not want to view a second image of them, one I will commit to memory. They're testing me, of course, as we used to test teachers when I was here. One time I pretended not to know basic facts about American history on a new teacher's first day of school. Carson was horrified. The teacher was quite young like I am now, without the added benefit of ever having taught in an independent school. The trick was to be hyper-confident despite my pretend lack of knowledge so the teacher would feel bad about correcting me too deliberately. Others joined in. The first twenty minutes of class the teacher wrapped himself in a pretzel, trying to avoid hurting our feelings or making us look stupid, even though we placed Ben Franklin in the 1890s. One student made a bold move to feign difficulty recalling whether we ever had a civil war in America. Disrespect towards a teacher is like a waterfall: once he falls over the edge, he's flying all the way down without anyone else's help, and by the end of the fall, the centrifugal force builds, hurdling toward a splash that surfaces far larger than anything capable from the initial drop. When we tricked that teacher, I had looked over at Carson halfway between a classmate's description of how the Civil Rights Movement caused the Great Depression; Carson watched the teacher begin to stutter as our classmate became more and more sure of himself, Carson's eyes betraying pity beneath his vacant stare, his weakness evident even then. No one's going to do the same to me.

Sit on the edge of the stage, my old stage, at 3:30 sharp. I dismiss the English class I sub for three minutes early in order to achieve maximum possession of the auditorium as the brand new improv group begins. The first cohort of kids: three girls and two guys—probably sophomores—arrive talking to each other with barely a look in my direction. Classic—total indifference achieved.

Next come two slender senior girls; their posture and Under Armour pullovers suggest athletes rather than theater people. If the seniors are here, maybe they've already cleared the first hurdle of doubt and are keeping an open mind. After all, it's about time a teacher with sketch comedy ability showed up at this school. The same two guys who shoved me earlier stroll in and begin chatting up the two girls as they take their seats in the front row. No other way to look at this development than as a setback: no one sits in the front row except troublemakers.

A junior girl with flowing red hair walks in assured with a crooked posture. Her curls dangle a little past her shoulders. She wears army fatigue pants. We never got a casual dress day when I was in school.

Three guys tentatively keep their eyes to the floor as they make their way down the long ramp to the third row, lavishing in their perceived awkwardness—probably freshmen.

It dawns on me that I should have come up with a cool opening improv task, something to grab their attention, something to focus on them meeting each other instead of greeting me and my own unease. I resent what most of these kids are projecting outwardly, a vague skeptical air combined with indifference, but the thing to consider is they're here. If I can keep them here, and if they return, I'm on my way to a permanent position at the school. Declan Sullivan, the overeager guy who got me to sign the paperwork for this club, takes a seat in the second row and nods to me. I've assured the kid I'll let him in on leadership stuff later in this session. One more student enters from the side. She carries herself with a deliberate stance, her shoulder propped in a confident, controlled posture, maybe another athlete. Think she's in the junior English class I subbed for; I should really learn everyone's names faster. Takes a seat, third-row center where she feigns some light skepticism my way.

I rise and look out at all of them as I stand downstage in a centered position. I remember standing in the same spot sophomore year during tryouts for *Robin Hood*. Carson and I both wanted the Sherriff of Nottingham. Mom should have done a better job of convincing him not to try out for the role; he was too whiny, and I was perfect. Neither of us got it, though the damage was done once I gave my monologue in terms of which of the two twin brothers was a stronger actor.

"Thanks for coming to Improv Club," I tell the kids. "I know that most of the clubs are completely student-run, and this club will be eventually, but I do bring some unique skills to the school, and I would like to teach you some of those skills, so you'll be able to teach others and run this thing on your own."

"At which point we won't need you anymore," the aggressive kid who shoved me says. A few of the sophomores shift in their seats uncomfortably; perhaps taunting is not a natural state of being for these kids.

"Maybe not," I say. I shouldn't have broached that scenario. Why didn't I introduce myself and provide my background first? I've got to get out of this rabbit hole of weakness. "Give me a place," I say with an edge in my voice.

"What?" the bully kid says.

"A place," I say. "Give me a place."

"The North Pole," the bully's friend says.

"Now a profession. Give me a profession."

"Does it need to relate to the North Pole?" the redhead asks.

"It does not."

"An airline pilot," she says.

"Okay. Now I need a scenario."

"Penguins!" one of the senior girls says.

"That's good, but there needs to be some obstacle in regards to penguins. Then you'll have a scenario."

"They're in danger," she says.

I look out at everyone. "How are the penguins in danger?" Some of the kids whisper to each other, productive whispering, brainstorming whispering. I should have started with this activity.

"The penguins want to start a band," the bully kid says.

"Okay, and it's dangerous to start a band, right?" A few laughs and nods from the younger group that came in; they know this is supposed to be somewhat entertaining. "So we've got an airline pilot flying over the North Pole where some penguins are busy starting a band."

"You've got to figure out your priorities," the redhead says.

"It's true," I say. "Lots of pitfalls at the North Pole, but overall, if you want to start a band, you should start that thing and forget about the freezing temperatures."

A few kids laugh. I better get this scenario moving fast. Remember your own time in high school. They did not appreciate how clever you were. Your moment to shine is now. Assert how it should have been. "Coming in for a landing; cruising altitude to 20,000 feet...above the North Pole! Control tower, do you come in? Control tower do you copy? This is Captain McQuinn, requesting permission to land with the remainder of the Christmas presents on special order. Do you copy? It appears no one is in the control tower? Elves, are you there? I say, elves, do you copy? Oh, gosh, something's wrong with one of the engines. I need to reach the elves right away."

Their attention is still fixed on me. Made it this far. My muscles relax ever so slightly. "Any penguins out there? This is North Pole Airlines requesting permission to land on North Pole Runway Number 3. Could a brave Emperor Penguin please come forward? Your assistance is needed immediately." I spread my arms out like wings and glide across the stage, moving from stage right to stage left and back again, complete with airplane humming sounds. I hear a few chuckles from the audience; I press on. "I really need a brave penguin out there, one who knows how to fly a medium-range aircraft. One who has particularly good eyesight and can handle a descending velocity from 20,000 feet."

Now I steal a glance at them. My eyes make an imploring look that says, "this is your cue."

"What kind of landing gear do you have?" the girl from my English class asks.

"Standard grade."

She glances at the students around her. "Think that will do."

A few of them laugh. I smile, gesturing for her to join me on stage.

She rises from her seat and does.

"Is this Paulie? Paulie the *Penguin*?" I ask.

"It is," she says as she takes the stage five feet in front of me.

"This is Captain McQuinn. I'm so relieved you answered. The engines are giving way, and I need to land now. Can you guide me to the runway?"

"Of course. Though as soon as we finish, I need to get back to starting my band."

More chuckles. She picked up on a key detail and continued with it, a deft move.

"Yes, I imagine there's many hurdles to starting your band, what with the group dynamics, the songwriting, and then there's the marketing on top of it, but Paulie... Can you tell me which direction to turn the plane?"

"Due east. Is your landing gear up?"

"It is now." I make a landing gear sound that comes off like a cyborg starting a latte machine. A few more kids laugh. This is so much better than when I was in high school.

The girl cups her right hand above her eyes as she stares down our imagined runway. "I can see you descending. Take it slow and easy; focus on the red candy cane front and center."

"Check. Will do. Your *details* are really helping me to land. Paulie, as soon as I land, I can help you start that band."

"That's great news, Mr. Levinson—I mean Captain..."

"McQuinn."

"Captain McQuinn!"

"Land that plane, McQuinn," someone yells from the house.

My arms, which carry the weight of this extensive improv, drop to a "landing position." "Landing in three, two, one."

"Welcome to the North Pole," she says. "Look out for that candy cane."

I make a few evasive maneuvers, just missing the imaginary candy cane.

The students clap from the house.

"Let's give Paulie the Penguin a hand." The girl returns to the house. I take a seat on the edge of the stage. "Look," I say to everyone. "I'm Mr. Levinson, and I was a student here a little while ago. I'm not going to pretend that I was popular or anything like that. I had friends: my twin brother was here with me, but we didn't rule the school or anything. Everyone is here today because somewhere underneath, there's a desire to perform. I'd never say the words, 'make a fool of one's self.' Only someone who doesn't know the power of performance would say such a stupid thing. There is a special kind of power to improvisation. If you can think of what to say on the fly, you can do anything. I will show you how to do this once a week. Then you can start to lead the meetings. What do you think?"

Surprisingly, a warmth swells from the audience, rises toward the stage. Validation and gradual acceptance cut through the air. It's deceptive because at first the approval comes off more potent than it should. My confidence increases, strengthening a fragility that's always there, gnawing away. For a moment, they listened to me without worrying what quip they would make next; without focusing on the depths of their own insecurities, which I imagine are substantial despite their successful ability to project I'm the odd one out, which I am.

Declan Sullivan shakes his head and leaves in a huff. I

wonder what's wrong.

The guy who shoved me in the hall raises his hand. "When are we going to meet again?" he asks.

"One week," I say.

The next day, this same guy nods to me in the narrow English wing as I head to my first class. I pass another classroom, and the freshmen from improv nod in approval from their desks. The student who participated in the improv stands with a friend alongside the lockers and beams. "Mr. Levinson, I just wanted to tell you how we appreciated the Penguin improv yesterday."

I thank her. Horace, a middle-aged history teacher who I used to call Mr. Toms when I was a student here, gestures at me. I follow Toms to his classroom across the hall. He shuts the door. I look up at him and see the concern, the weariness, which rests underneath his brown eyes. His expression beckons me to make some kind of admittance of fault. He leads with his beard, which now has grown gray streaks running up each side since the time I was his student. "How was sketch club last night?" he asks.

"Think it went pretty well."

"My advisee said you really need to get more people involved."

That sounds insane considering I had solid numbers for my first outing. "It was only the first meeting," I say.

"Yes, but the kids are supposed to do the organizing. It's not a class. My advisee said you were on stage the whole time. You didn't give anyone else a chance."

"Who's your advisee?"

"It doesn't matter."

"They saw how to do improv on stage, in front of an

audience."

"It's not about you, Sebastian."

I don't remember ever informing my advisor about another teacher, especially over something so trivial. I'm sure other kids did, but it's hard to believe a teacher would go and carry out their advisee's complaints like some directive emanated from on high. Wentworth's excitement over my alumni status may not reflect back on the students.

"Thanks for the tip," I tell Horace. I smile and move toward the door.

"You can watch me teach anytime you like," he says.

MOIRA

1995

STANDING AT THE front of my parents' double gallery house on Nashville Street on an early June day, I watch Victor's Audi disappear from view for the last time 'til Thanksgiving will arrive. He will head off to the University of Chicago for a summer program and then the start of school. I will stay local. What looks like a significant obstacle will become a natural part of our courtship. Striding up the porch steps, my shoes almost kick my mother's geraniums for lack of attention. Dropping my balance, my purse slops loose, dangling just above the wooden floor. Inside, Father and Mother sit on the couch dressed up: Mom in a sky-blue cocktail dress, my father in a navy sport coat and paisley tie. Both of them can't look away from Raymond, who leans back in our easy chair possessing a confidence not unlike the night I met him, yet more reserved, more probing. I glance at my mother, unsure what I should say besides hello, disturbed she seems so far away. Her eyes betray neither understanding nor agreement to the conversation they are in the middle of.

"Take a seat, Moira," she says matter-of-factly. "This

is Raymond Alders. He says you met him at the party you went to a few weeks ago." I register the hate rising from inside her throat. She does not want this guest in her house, yet at the same time, will do nothing to accelerate his exit. "He has an opportunity for you and wants to run it by us first."

My father tries to smile at Raymond, who dismisses the gesture as unworthy of his acknowledgment. I remain standing. Do not want this to go on any longer than it has to.

"A position came open in The Society. Let's call it an internship," Raymond says.

"Is that what it is?" my mother says. "Or what you'd like to call it?"

"Internship. Opportunity. All the same, really."

"What do you want me to do?" I ask. The question seems rude as soon as it escapes my lips; I have disrupted his chicanery and misdirection.

"We require bookkeeping assistance," he says too comfortably.

"Bookkeeping?" I say. There is an underlying danger in his simplicity.

Raymond radiates relief; he is ready to throw his offer out in the open where it can propel me toward him. "It's also a scholarship," he adds.

"For college?" I ask.

"Yes, for college," my father says, rather pleased. "The Society will fund your studies for the next four years."

"For my bookkeeping," I reiterate.

"We will orient you to the inner workings of The Society as well," Raymond says.

I keep my eyes fixed on Mother, struggling to avoid Raymond's prying gaze. If anyone can get me out of this, it's her.

"Everything is settled, Moira. Raymond wanted to tell you in person with us here," my father says. Or did they insist he tell me with them present? Raymond looks over at me and smiles genially. My father beams in his presence. Raymond possesses the ability to make a man feel as if he were in an exclusive club, which of course, in this case, my father is.

My mother crosses her legs, maybe in defiance. She can see what my father doesn't, what I could the night of the party. Raymond is not the leader of The Society by coincidence. His controlled demeanor keeps something far more sinister and dangerous at bay. My mother resents our reliance on Raymond, and I resent them for their capitulation. He has to be supplying something for her cancer, something in the realm of the unusual: I am the bargaining chip.

"She can begin next week," Raymond says with a flourish. He waits to catch my glance. I avoid it for as long as I can, but when this is no longer possible, it is as if he blows a part of himself into a bellow of smoke in my direction. Since Victor possesses a potent ability, it is challenging not to endeavor what Raymond's is. He is about to answer the question.

"What do you think of the deal," he says, but doesn't. He smiles as my father describes the inside of his favorite omelet choice at Camilla Grill. Not a sound escapes Raymond's lips. My mouth hangs open, the saliva dry and course.

"It's okay. You're not hearing things," he seems to

say. This time he looks at me as he "speaks."

"You can hear me?" I cover my mouth but no words have escaped. How did I do that?

"Of course I heard you."

"I can do this?"

"It appears you can."

"Why should I work for you?"

"Your mother. I'm going to help her."

"I'm not a pawn."

"There's a lot you don't know. That's where the internship comes in."

"Moira, are you all right?" my mother asks.

My attention returns to the live sound in front of me. I nod. Imagine an older Victor, owning the room as Raymond does. Suddenly both men are too much for me to handle. Yet, as my father moves on to describing the texture of crust on his ideal key lime pie, I realize there is little choice but to steer through an impending storm.

A week after Raymond visits my family, a large manila envelope arrives in the mailbox; I know it's for me before I see my name in green block printing. Take the silver letter opener from the third drawer in the kitchen and slice it open. Cardboard backing sticks to the top. Mom lurks in the doorway, wearing her puffy pink bathrobe. It is Sunday. There is never mail on Sunday.

"What is it?" she says.

"An acceptance letter. To Tulane."

She just shakes her head and exits.

I follow her into the living room. "Where are you going?" I call out, but she is already through the door to the back porch to confront my father. The air is sticky thin; I gulp more of it in to compensate for my anxiety over what my mother might say.

Mom stands in front of Father, who lounges on the porch swing reading *The Times-Picayune*. She waits 'til he looks up.

"I thought she was going to UNO," Mom says.

"Isn't she?"

I join her with the manila envelope. She takes it from me, clutching the thick bundle of a possible future with force.

"Not according to this."

He drops the paper on the bench and snatches the envelope from her. After reading the acceptance letter, all he can do is smile.

"Looks like Moira got in."

"I didn't know she applied."

"I didn't," I say.

He continues to read, trying not to grimace. After finishing the letter, he moves to the next document, which I already see is a housing application.

"Well," my mom finally says.

"Would she live on campus?"

"I could live here to save money, just like I was going to do at the other school," I say. I am already dreaming of the oak tree-lined campus, the 150-year-old classrooms that emit scents of must and chalk: so many intellectual connections and *a-hah!* moments to enjoy over the next four years.

"I know a history professor there—young guy—just got his doctorate," Father says.

My mother is not amused by his ignoring the larger issue. "Oliver, she didn't apply." She looks at me for final clarification. "You sure you didn't apply?"

"I didn't."

She shakes her head at Father. "Doesn't that bother you?"

"Our daughter's been accepted to an excellent university."

"He did this, obviously," she says.

I sit down on the porch swing next to my father and clasp the envelope in my hand. They cannot tarnish this no matter how the argument ends. "I wanted to apply. I would have gotten in if I had applied. But we couldn't afford the tuition," I remind them. Other details are irrelevant.

"Gather it's been taken care of," Father says.

"So you knew about this?" I ask him.

Father shakes his head.

Mom glances at me, rubs her eyes. "He's going to want something in return, Moira." Her voice cracks. "If that doesn't bother you, it sure bothers me."

"He explained it to us. There will be an internship," Father says.

"You know it's more," Mom says. She tightens the band on her bathrobe. "What will you do when I won't be here to pick up the pieces?"

Father and I can do nothing but let the reality and gloom of her comment ooze into our pores. "Mom, this is the school I should be going to." Once, when I was supposed to be walking to Audubon Park, I instead snuck onto campus, pretending as though campus police might stop me any moment, as if a ten-year-old girl's inquisitiveness would be some type of threat to the scholarly environment unfolding on the main academic quad. They never stopped me. I sat at the coffee shop watching the freshmen girls gaze across the picnic table at the freshmen guys. Some of the girls looked across longingly; others stared with envy. At the time, I thought it was all longing, but there is a subtle difference. You can tell in the lips.

"We should not think about this opportunity as something arranged, something unseemly," Father says.

"I can handle him," I say. They both turn to me, surprised.

Mom places her hand on my head; what at first seems like a gesture of love is a display of sympathy at my naïveté. "How can you handle him, Moira, if your father cannot?"

Three weeks later and one week before I need to sign the university letter of commitment, he is standing on the streetcar tracks outside my high school. He taps his toes on the metal track, a gratuitous gesture at any age. He doesn't waste time as to why he is here. "Are you going to accept?" he asks. "You know the tuition will be covered. Think of it as a scholarship."

"Part of the internship," I offer.

"Exactly. I know your mother doesn't approve. That's something you will need to get over."

Did he desire for me to "get over" her after she passes?

"Internship doesn't begin for three years. Study up and enjoy yourself in the meantime."

"You haven't told me what the internship will entail."

"Why would I?"

Standing in the shadow of the oak trees that stretch for miles along Saint Charles, I realize my parents consented to him entering the front door. Once he is in the living room, he can put his feet up on the coffee table, so to speak, listen to some CDs and take his sweet time, which he is well on the way to doing. "I like to know what's ahead of me," I finally say when I can no longer stand his silence.

"When you lack the answer to such questions, you approach what's ahead in a vastly different manner."

"Maybe."

"You will enjoy college," he says.

"I know I will."

The grating of the streetcar's wheels against the metal track grow louder as it scuttles closer. In a moment, he'll escape for the next three years. In a moment, a tuition payment and a promise will be all he'll leave me with. He looks down the tracks at the approaching streetcar and smirks. He leaves me with the smile of a father figure—an insincere gesture on his part.

MOIRA

1998

IN THE SUMMER approaching my senior year, I secure an internship downtown off Canal at the Federal District Attorney's office for Southern Louisiana. Answer phones, route calls, and take voracious notes, which is the best part since I am able to get a real glimpse inside the legal maneuverings the prosecuting attorneys take part in. Seriously considering applying to law school; the attorney's office is a trial run. Mother's former colleagues help me obtain the internship.

I become numb to the legal maneuverings behind the scenes. The prosecuting attorneys try to cut deals because they do not want to spend the time and resources on a case, even though it is often clear they could win if they dedicate themselves to a trial.

I recount one particular case to my friend Jean over drinks at a bar on Dauphine Street. The attorneys opt against taking a sex trafficker to trial; I become jaded about the whole affair. Jean nods with enthusiastic agreement, pointing out that if the department possessed further resources, they wouldn't need to cut so many deals. We toast to that statement, both laughing and proclaiming we would not hesitate to expose the injustices of society in the coming years. Jean's eyes then reveal a blurry exhaustion, her cheeks flush, her forehead wet with uncertainty.

My hand covers hers. Leaning over her, my voice emanates concern at her exhaustion. "What's wrong?" I ask. "You look awful."

"I feel worse."

"We should get you home."

Hold her hand as we trek down Dauphine, heading toward Decatur, where she lives in a walkup above a fish restaurant. The streets are generally safe this early in the evening, but I maintain a circulating gaze on foot. Jean's physical state becomes progressively worse as we turn down Toulouse, but she rallies once we hit Decatur, enough so I can leave her in the safety of her apartment to sleep off whatever she has taken ill with.

Step onto the busy street; the glare of car headlights bounces off my dress. I encounter the sinking feeling I am now alone for the remainder of the evening, and I shouldn't be. How does Jean's condition deteriorate so quickly, but then recover enough that a hospital visit seems superfluous? While waiting for the streetlight to turn, I see him—leaning against the welcoming wall of the Nightingale Hotel, checking his watch as if he were expecting me, and I am moderately late. He wears a black windbreaker over his button-down, his hair now containing whisks of gray and white that stand out of place in the light wind. Am not sure if I should smile or run, yet I remember his patronage, the reason I retain the connections in the first place to sit in a bar on a stifling summer night, lobbing complaints over the inherent injustices of our legal system. I cross the street into the heart of danger I had agreed to.

"You're not late, but you're not early," he says with a touch of anxiousness. His ability to appear completely threatening must have dissipated over time or he is unable to mask his anticipation of whatever he is about to embark on with me. "You look cold," he says as I step onto the ancient pavement, no longer separated by the safety Decatur offers.

"You look older," I say.

"I think your friend will be all right," he offers.

My shoulders tense. His lips clamp down, confirming his subterfuge.

"You could have called me. I would have come," I say.

"I needed to be sure."

"Don't do that again."

"Fine for you to make pronouncements, but the greater question you're pondering is how did I do it?"

"I hold no interest in becoming a magician."

"I have no interest in one working for me."

"Does Victor know you're here?" I know the likely answer is no, but I want him to confirm it.

"I suspect he's in his dorm room in Chicago, reading late into the night." Victor was away for the summer busy with a government internship of his own. Surprising Raymond sanctioned such an opportunity. He turns and begins walking south toward Canal. I watch for a moment before following him. "In order for The Society to function," he says, "we require multiple businesses to generate income on a regular basis. One of those businesses is tourism."

"You give tours?"

"One of my favorite ways to create income."

"You have more than a few competitors."

"Not for the type of tour we conduct," he says. I find myself surprised to be following him, even though I agreed to—even though I suspect some degree of harm will come to me in time with his companionship.

A subtle *ding* from an old clock sounds inside his pocket. He checks the source, a silver watch no doubt over a hundred years old. I imagine he is also this old, some kind of vampire trapped in a middle-aged man's body. If that is true, both Victor and I could be in for a reckoning we have zero control over.

He stares toward the Mississippi; the river smells of wet plastic and tar. Raymond squints his nose as if he smells it too. "We have an appointment with a young couple in a few minutes. Tonight's tour."

"Only one couple?"

"These are expensive tours. I would not waste my time with anything less."

"Must be quite expensive to make it worth your while."

He smiles.

"What are you going to show them?"

"Watch and learn," he says as if I would be able to mimic anything he does with some kind of recitation.

I know we are not alone even before the young man makes his presence known to us. Perhaps five years older than myself, his beautiful tan linen suit is a clear sign of his wealth. His companion, a lovely brunette who looks my age, shifts from side to side anxiously, attempting to shield her nervous energy she is used to concealing. I can't possibly imagine what type of "tour" Raymond plans to take us on.

Raymond grins at both of them with suspicious positivity. "Welcome to Calhoun Street Tours. You possess the payment I presume?"

The man hands Raymond a filled envelope. Raymond runs his hand over the envelope, smiles with satisfaction. "Let's be off," he says.

The three of us follow him back up Decatur, heading for Jackson Square. The more official tours are winding down at this late hour. Ghost tours and vampire tours are the standard, usually led by a mysterious fellow and part-time actor in his fifties or sixties, someone with a raspy gray beard requiring a trim and wearing a cape or a turned-up coat collar—perhaps both. The tour guides always seem dressed for the occasion as opposed to Raymond, who appears primed for a shareholder's meeting minus the windbreaker.

The woman keeps her eyes on the architecture and the garbage in the streets as if she is taking in the Quarter for the first time. "Why is it so dirty?" she asks.

Raymond smiles to himself as if no one has asked a question. "So much scandal over time, the city realizes there's no point in washing it down."

"How far is our destination?" the man asks.

"Only two blocks," Raymond answers, mildly perturbed.

"I still don't understand how this works," the man says.

"That's hardly your responsibility," Raymond says.

The man's female companion nods, indicating she agrees and feels indignation that her partner would offer such an ill-advised comment. "We're looking forward to what you have to show us," she affirms.

This seems to put Raymond at ease just as we arrive at the corner of St. Philip and Chartres. I haven't said anything during the entire walk to our destination and feel I should add something before becoming completely invisible. Just then, Raymond places his warm hand on my arm, indicating that it is okay; that no additional contribution will be necessary.

Raymond stands at the corner, his black boot almost digging into the concrete like a pitcher preparing to throw a fast ball. His gaze fixes on the green front door of a worn-down building on the other side of the street. The white pillars, which crust over, recall a residence once inhabited by occupants of significant means. Raymond takes in the residence with the man and woman standing on either side of him. I stand a few feet behind them, Raymond's loyal second. Lights beside the front door shine back at us, eliminating the idea that this dwelling is solely a relic from the past. Our silence hints at something darker; it is clear we have already reached our destination for the tour.

"I suppose we cannot go inside," the man says.

"They've let it go to pieces," remarks the woman. Garbage bags full of overflowing sticks lay along the front walkway. A cherry-shaded lamp shimmers in the darkness, alerting any passerby that people do reside here and are focused on the business of living their lives.

"I want to leave," the woman decides.

"We didn't come here for defeat," the man says evenly.

"It's not some game," she says.

I wait on Raymond for direction, to fill us in on the

plan, at least to do something to calm them as circumstances seem to be escalating to some place I have no access to.

"You did not come here for closure." He clears his throat. "If that's what you want, I suggest we leave now," Raymond says.

The woman takes a step toward the house. Her nose eases forward, just enough to imply that if left to her own devices, she would knock on the front door. "No, we didn't come for that," she says.

"This is the point of the tour where I offer you an out. I am happy to refund half the price for the evening. Once we begin, I plan to finish."

The man glances at the woman; her expression reassures him—leaving will not be an option.

"That won't be necessary," he says.

Raymond relaxes his shoulders as he closes his eyes. Whatever he is doing, it is beginning. The front lights cut to black, so only the faint glow from the café around the corner lights our way. I cover myself instinctively; can sense the temperature drop. Breaths become shallow, trapped underground, making us lightheaded from the inside. Raymond opens his eyes. "He's still in there. He never left."

A gasp emits from the woman. "He's trapped?"

Raymond pays her no mind and continues right on. "The other family is ignorant to his presence. He's seen to that."

"He's aware enough to take precaution?" the man asks.

"I want to go inside," the woman says.

Raymond closes his eyes again. "Quiet. He spends his

days switching off between the parlor and his old room. He wanders between them as if each holds the answer to his question. Restless, missing something ethereal, right out of reach—each day a struggle to find it, though he never does."

"My baby."

Raymond glimpses the woman but concentrates on the house. "He tolerates the new occupants, though doesn't much care for them. They have a younger son—almost two: the age he used to be. He tries not to be jealous; sometimes it is difficult not to be, especially when the boy receives presents on his birthday or on Christmas. Like the videogame, which becomes a fascination and also a rumination on what is now lost, what will never be found. He considers leaving, many times throughout a given day, but he's pulled between his dreams and the wandering. He's beckoned back to the two rooms."

"Tell him he can leave," says the man.

Raymond ignores him. "The parlor is where it happened. He knows this. It doesn't haunt him. Not exactly, but the parlor remains a puzzle with no good exits. When he's there, there's a comfort of familiarity as it's the place he needed to cling to when it first happened, before he was allowed to broaden his horizons within the rest of the house." Raymond tips his ear like he is listening to someone, waiting for his turn to speak. "He knows we're here."

The woman reaches for the man like a life jacket at sea. He grimaces at her.

"He's glad you've come," Raymond trudges on. "He wonders why you're no longer with him."

"Tell him we miss him," says the man.

Raymond shakes his head. "But then he remembers, and he remembers the parlor. He wishes he could play games with you. Sometimes he takes things, things that belong to the current occupants: watches, key fobs, receipts they meant to save. He thinks it's funny. They do not think it's funny of course, but what he's really doing is imagining the items belong to you, and that he is playing a game. With you. Sometimes late in the morning, he realizes what happened to him. Not for long as the haze sets in. Yet, for a brief interval, he does remember. He wonders why he was left alone in the parlor, why you decided to lay his high chair in the isolated place, away from the goings-on of the kitchen, away from the place you yourselves sat down to eat. This isn't a place where people eat, he thinks. Why doesn't he get to eat near Mommy and Daddy?"

The woman steps back in the street in disarray. She turns to run, but no direction seems viable. She staggers. I grab her and hold on.

"No one heard him. No one heard him for so very long. He cried and cried, his screams a doomed siren in an abandoned town. His tiny hands gripping the high chair for dear life. He presumes there was a reason, but he does not pretend to understand because he does not understand. He grasps, in his own way, how busy you both were, how stressed with work you felt during dinner hours. Sometimes he seizes on these understand-ings when they come to him before the haze. But he doesn't really know work, what it means to do those things. Sometimes he becomes a more advanced age he missed the opportunity to experience. He grows irritable of the other occupants; feels less connected to them because he feels less connected to the house and considers leaving again. He wants you to know he will decide to leave one day, during these moments of exasperation." Raymond turns to the woman. "Would you like to see one of these moments?" he asks her.

She nods, resolute again.

"He does not guarantee a cheerful vision. He wants you to be aware of that beforehand."

"I understand," she says.

Raymond steps back and takes hold of the woman's arm with a smooth maneuver. He makes eye contact with the woman for the first time since arriving at the house, a look of warning more than anything else, the only reassurance evident on his face to let her know the experience is real, that all of it is happening before his eyes, and it is about to happen before hers. His hands reach for her shoulders; I'm sure she can feel the warmth radiating from them. For a moment there is nothing—time left on ice. Then she gasps. He struggles to help her stay balanced. My gaze remains fixed on the front door, trying to imagine what it is the woman is seeing. Whatever it is, both Raymond and the woman are now on some other plane, holding onto a loose phantom that will haunt the woman for years.

"I see him," she finally says. "Oh, God, I see him."

Raymond grips her shoulders harder. "Do not look away."

"How could I?"

Uncertain exactly what she sees, but from what I sense on my own, the woman witnesses her little boy in his mid-teen years. The woman sees her child thrash and kick inside an impossibly large high chair, large enough to hold a teenager, his teenager arms dangling and helpless. Then of course the chair topples over. From what I gather, these are not the exact circumstances they find the boy in when he is two—there is more to it than that, but some echo exists in what the woman witnesses while Raymond holds her, viewing the same image. I know the woman observes more than she lets on. I suspect it is worse than anything Raymond describes out loud to us. When it is over, Raymond lets her go. The woman vomits on the pavement. The man watches, perhaps jealous of her experience, but overall not truly envying her in the least.

The woman picks herself up, her knees dirty from kneeling on the ground. She nods to Raymond; his shoulders slacken. A tension in the air subsides. The connection evaporates. The woman tugs on Raymond's coat like a child asking if she could stay longer. "There's more you have to show me. Something else."

Raymond evades her gaze. "Why do you think that is?"

"We need to keep going," she says.

"That goes without saying."

"Show me."

Raymond gives her his hand.

The man and I stand on in absentia, as if our exchanging glances masks the helplessness in the air.

I look closer into Raymond's eyes; they transition to an orangy red, a star burning toward a white dwarf. Whatever it is that Raymond sees, the woman begins to picture the same thing. Raymond guides her hand 'til she touches something indecipherable to the man and me.

"Will this happen?" she asks.

"If you let it," Raymond says.

"Will he want it to happen?"

"I cannot tell."

When it is over, the man and woman leave us on the corner. They walk north toward the Marigny. We start back toward Decatur. I know Raymond performed a service to the couple, something I would not have imagined earlier in the evening. The usefulness of that service is something else entirely.

"Do you think you helped them?" I ask as we move through a nearly vacant and undisturbed Jackson Square.

"I did more than what was asked."

"That's not the same thing."

He stops at the river and scales the concrete walkway to look down on the murky water.

"What did you show her at the end?"

"What do you think I showed her?"

"Another child."

Raymond's nondenial functions as an affirmation.

"Is it real?" I say.

"Might be.

"You have the ability to project that?"

"I'm not the only one."

I am almost sure he is alluding to Victor, but maybe he isn't. "How do you know she won't tell her husband what she saw?"

"Would you?" Gleeful menace punctuates his words.

Curiosity gets the best of me. "What kind of tasks do you want me to complete on this internship?"

Raymond smiles, surprised. He looks out at the Mississippi. A dark ripple forms, a black swirl of dull water and oil. "You're probably wondering what we do with our funds," he says. "Why I do not escalate things if I possess such a gift. I'll tell you this: there's not enough of us to do so. Most of The Society are just that—a lineage connected by blood and privilege. Some like myself, like perhaps young Victor; we hold the rest up. Perhaps you will too."

"I only want to help my mother."

He places his hand on my bare arm, his skin smoothing my few black hairs in a downward motion. I find my fingers pointing at the ripple in the river.

"Close your eyes," he says.

Instead of multiplying the ripple in the river, I expect something else will occur, something residing in my subconscious, some ability about to reveal itself; all I need to do is wait. The wind picks up. Can smell his breath on my lips and nose. Pine and cane sugar settles into the air. His hand rests on my waist.

"What are you doing?" I say. Then I see it. We are someplace else, in a garden filled with magnolias and petunias. Pungent odors overpowering. Birth and death, the whole life cycle taking place beneath our feet. My hair contains silver streaks. We stroll arm and arm, my weight shifting with a different center of gravity than the one I embody by the Mississippi. He is older, wrinkles cracking underneath his eyes; he moves slower—white hair blows over his forehead.

"It's us," I say. "You're showing me the future?" In the garden, he takes my left hand. The black hair on the back of his hand is now white. My right hand holds onto another's, a teenager's. It is a young, firm grip, belonging to a male.

"Who is that?"

"You are doing this, by the way."

"There's no way."

"You are the one projecting it."

"Is it the future?"

"Could be."

"Who is the child?" I ask. As soon as the words leave my mouth, I know the child is mine. The garden departs my field of vision. The child unlatches the lock on a fence, and the three of us cross the barrier together into an optimistic sun. A jubilant warmth stretches out over a vast field, casting a shining glow on our faces. I hold the child's hand tighter because I want to, not out of any danger or uncertainty. Yet, back on the bank of the Mississippi, I feel uncertainty now: uncertainty over my internship, my career path, and most of all, uncertainty regarding the man in the black windbreaker whose gaze is locked upon the sporadic ripples in the water even though I know he is silently ascertaining my feelings and motives from moment to moment.

"What do you want with me?" I finally say after my field of vision reverts to the wet wind and the scents of oil wafting from the river.

"Stay in the fold. Learn what you can."

"What do you plan to teach me?"

"Staying in the fold means not asking questions like that." He scoops up a pebble and tosses it across the water, watching it skip away from us and into the dark night. "This would be a different position than your significant other occupies. And in case you were wondering, our arrangement that was settled must be maintained. You are not to discuss any dealings with him." He nods with practiced authority as if this plan is the key to some kind of higher purpose and not at all an opportunity to take advantage of a young woman. His gesture is ironic considering he affords a glimpse of some possible future in which a child exists that is likely his. I think of my mother, reflecting on the supposed aid he is in the process of providing. My mother, who lacks any true alternatives to the cancer waiting for her in the wings, has already sanctioned my interactions with this man. It is up to me to embark on whatever he deems essential.

Eventually, a man's ethos reveals itself. He cannot help it. If he longs to let you in, only total immersion will suffice. An effective enigma fashions others' perception of him. The picture he yearns to paint for his mentee is a different one. One morning finds us standing on opposite sides of Royal Street. There is an uncertainty of how he will guide me through his personal rabbit hole. He clearly relishes the opportunity to flaunt his talents. Our obstacles might be self-inflicted. Raymond's voice reaches my side of the street, slipping above and underneath the scents of melon and stale gum. "Time to see how the frosting's made," he says. He extends his hand, beckoning me to walk to him. For all I know, our errand might be found via my side of the street, but there is no way he will cross to me. I join him only after determining I still want to. We walk north, all the way to Esplanade. Cross back to my side of the street within half a block.

Esplanade takes on a different shade in Raymond's

presence compared to the times I venture to its bars and jazz clubs with friends during college. The sprawling oak trees shield us momentarily from reality, allowing Raymond to craft his own. He somehow succeeds in facilitating my budding anticipation; he refuses to reveal where we are heading or what our purpose will be. I suspect it will be mildly sinister; otherwise, why wait until now to show me? However, Raymond remains calm, even downright cheery. We turn down Burgundy Street. He clears debris in the road without touching it, his brazenness building as we near our destination.

"When we go inside," he says, "let me do the talking. And the probing."

"The probing?"

He purses his lips. "You'll see. And don't worry; you'll get your chance."

We reach a sky-blue shotgun house in need of a new coat of paint. Raymond turns the doorknob, eschewing any knock. The living room we enter nearly slumps in Raymond's presence; its vaulted ceilings slouch with lukewarm mildew coating, the dry paint dangling amid the musty ventilation. A vaguely familiar, cleanshaven man in his early thirties with wandering eyes enters the room, greets Raymond as if they were old friends from college. A dash of desperation colors the man's gestures. "You're right on time," he says.

"So are you."

"It's my house."

Raymond smirks in my direction. "This is a guy who gets things done."

"I try," the man says.

"And you do."

The man sizes me up in the friendliest way he can muster even though it is still a failure. "Who is this?" he says to Raymond.

"My assistant." It is the first time Raymond employs that title. The man's demeanor changes. He must realize that if Raymond chose to bring me, something lays in waiting beneath the friendly feeling Raymond fosters.

"Clifford Lomax," the man says to me. "Let's sit at the table." I remember now where I have seen the man before: on local television—at the press conference after our most recent hurricane. He is the mayor's right-hand man. "So why are you visiting my home today?" he asks.

"Stop calling it your home; we both know you don't live here." Raymond points at Clifford. "You know full well why I've come."

"Raymond, your proposal was discussed at length with the city council members."

"And?"

"And ultimately, I couldn't sway them. The other offer on the table was simply too good."

Raymond considers what Clifford said. He catches a whiff of his own fingers. "Do you like to go out to eat?"

Clifford's face lights up. "Of course I like to go out to eat."

"Your favorite dish? Your favorite place?"

"Remoulade. At Antoine's."

Raymond wets his teeth with his tongue. "The texture of shrimp remoulade—delicate, watery but still savory."

"Exactly. Remoulade. Crawfish. The lifeblood of the city."

"I am so glad you feel that way, Clifford." Raymond turns to me. "When you get him alone, he makes valid points, doesn't he?"

"Where are you going with this?" Clifford asks.

Raymond keeps his gaze on me. "Tell me why he's nervous."

I am skeptical he truly wants me to do what he suggests, but he gestures for me to take myself there. I close my eyes. Turn to Clifford. I see him despite the fact my eyes are closed. Rough skin on his cheeks lead to crusted lips; the inside of a parched throat, desolate—nicked sideways like a penny on a scratch lottery ticket. Move through the cavernous parts—into his head. An austere protection. Something he's hidden. He leaves the place locked up. Onlookers beware. Functions day-to-day with this manufactured locked door, pretending it isn't there when he speaks with folks, though he visits it often. Especially on longer evenings. My fingers drift for the lock. I open my eyes a little. He's watching me. An embarrassed grin? Does he know? Likely he does. The lock tightens; everything scrambles. Feet slip on the inside. I gasp, a catch in my throat. I'm pulled back from the underbelly.

Raymond exhales. "That was close, Moira," he says.

"What are you doing?" Clifford asks.

Raymond puckers his lips in a scolding motion. "Shut up." He closes his eyes as he shakes his head in amusement. He stretches his hand toward Clifford. Raymond mumbles at vanilla nothingness. He twists in the wet wind flowing inside Clifford's thoughts. Raymond's eyes open; they widen further: the sublime knowledge of recognition. "How is your family, Clifford?"

"They're fine."

"Yeah? Your children, Hannah and Erik? Your wife, Laura?"

An annoyance bubbles in Clifford's voice. "My family's fine."

"What about your other one?"

"What?"

"Your other family." Raymond smiles at me.

"I don't know what you're talking about."

"Your daughter, Jacqueline. Your wife, Dawn. Your other family. The one that lives in Jefferson Parish."

Clifford looks to me then back to Raymond.

"You almost found it, Moira," Raymond says. "He was certainly hiding it. Clifford, don't look so aghast. Everyone's hiding something. I'm a little surprised someone in your position would hide something that large, though. Then again, why should I be?"

Clifford's surefootedness detaches itself from the rest of him. "The oil company," he stammers.

"The oil company what? What about it?"

"The benefits they're offering the council. They're astronomical. Beyond generous."

"As I alluded, the number of restaurants in this city are astronomical. And I hold too many controlling interests in too many of those restaurants to play footsie with another oil spill sneaking through our water system."

"I understand."

"You do not. Otherwise you wouldn't let things escalate this far."

"What do you propose I do?"

"What a pathetic thing to say. You're the mayor's chief of staff. You tell me. Or I'm going to tell Hannah, Erik, and Laura about Jacqueline and Dawn."

Clifford's chair scrapes against the table leg. Up on his feet, his anxiety plunges through the wooden flooring.

His movements are turbulent, on the verge of wild.

The slightest concern manifests in Raymond. "Clifford, where are you going?"

"Everything is balanced. You know how hard it is to balance the way I do?"

"Come back to the table," Raymond says.

Raymond and I eye each other. Something is not right; we both sense it's about to get worse. Instead of worrying for the man, I begin to worry for myself. What kind of life does Raymond intend to show me? If I carry on like this, wielding pressure the way he does, how will I keep my future children safe? "You going to check on him?" I say with urgency in my voice.

Raymond shakes his head.

"He's in danger."

"Good."

"That he's in danger?"

He shakes his head again. "That you sense it."

And then we hear the hollow snap from the pulled trigger. It pulsates through the house, a final cry signaling we are alone, that Raymond cannot get to Clifford any longer. But he already has. Raymond rises from his seat. "The mayor, you'll see, is more pliable than this man."

MOIRA

2022

I STILL THINK of the mayor's chief of staff sometimes when I see two families, looking eerily similar at the Café Du Monde, sipping coffee at two tables—side by side. How did that man manage two of them? It's a challenge to manage my own family. Sebastian, for one, finally has a job; now he needs a match. Or so we're told to believe from tradition. Victor takes the lead. Why he suddenly honors his parental obligations after considerable neglect is a mystery. I should be thankful for any effort undertaken. It would be easier to secure a match for Carson as opposed to Sebastian for a number of reasons, the chief of which is Carson's intelligence and overall genuine persona—both qualities my other son lacks. Yet Sebastian is the one who's here. Speaking to my Sebastian for an extended period of time is like studying a giraffe. At first, you're a little in awe at the sight of the thing, but after a while, you crane your neck, contorting yourself in order to follow the creature. Some people find Sebastian charming. As his mother, I do wish I were one of those people, at least for an hour or two. My own abilities prevent such suspension of disbelief. I could say the same for Victor, but my man's head is too far off in the clouds to form any reasonably informed opinion. He fails to appreciate Carson either, or his sizable abilities—at this point, still unknown to Carson himself. When a child is tested, the memory ceases to remain.

Victor and I never discuss our sons' personalities—we don't need to. Even Victor knows Sebastian's ego will be an obstacle to matching him with one of the young ladies of The Society. My man concocts an unusual solution to our quandary, a solution I do not share. To prevent Sebastian from scaring a girl off with his overly large ego, which does not match up with his virtues—I'm sorry to say, Victor thinks it best to find someone Sebastian will have a harder time dominating. Seems like a sound idea until you consider: what kind of girl *is* that exactly?

Our answer comes in the form of Addison Liondale, Raymond's young niece. Her age difference from Sebastian: six years. Not going to stop traffic ten years on, but at present, it's a good deal older than my very young man. Victor believes the match is perfect for our aims. I'm skeptical—particularly because she could become a rival of Carson's if he ever decides to return home.

The girl meets us at our home one mid-November evening when the air's begun to cool, even though the humidity continues to sulk in the background like a petulant six-year-old about to knock over a decorative bowl. Addison's on the short side: a buoyant five-foot-four. She carries herself with a practiced authority that's neither self-conscious nor adroit. She lacks the capacity to modulate her own self-assurance. The girl looks us in the eyes without fear. Betrays a few too many teeth when she grins. I want to walk over and coach her, let her try those first impressions a second time. She considers herself an adult, and I suppose she is, though we won't afford the same courtesy to our own offspring. Sebastian's no adult.

We know the girl and her reputation. Her added years may offer Sebastian extensive exasperation—but Victor deems this an asset. "Sebastian needs to grow up," he says. "What better way than an everyday reminder from his potential mate?" Easy for the person who need not face the forthcoming barrage of criticism. Of course, there is the additional positive of keeping Addison in the family: she'll be less of a threat to Carson if she becomes one of us.

We lead her to the living room; the girl joins me on the leather couch. Her erect posture and the ease with which she looks up at me suggests she's not of Sebastian's generation or ilk. In another time, we would negotiate with her parents, but tonight, we negotiate with her. My heart splits a little when I consider my baby is not the prize. He is the constant, the reality in the matter.

Her focus turns to Victor then back to me. I can feel her conniption underneath the glossy sheen she endeavors for our benefit. I detect no abilities raging inside her, but that doesn't mean they're not there. The girl may not have discovered them yet.

"Where is he?" she asks.

"The other room," Victor answers. He leans against the ornate fireplace we have never ignited.

"Have you ever met him?" I ask.

"Once," she says. "When he was in high school."

Victor and I exchange glances.

"I went to see the play his school put on."

"He was the lead," I say with unexpected pride.

"*Guys and Dolls*—I know. We spoke afterwards. I was a year out of college."

"I liked him in that play," Victor says.

"I'm excited to see him again," she says without the degree of actual excitement that should accompany such a statement.

"Why do you want to marry my son?" I ask.

Victor glares at me—like I care. I want to hear the answer, whatever it may be.

"It's time," she says. "It's time for me to be married."

Victor seems pleased by this answer. I am not. Then again, what do I really expect from such a match?

"That's not to say I don't find your son attractive," she says. "I do. From the available bachelors connected to our world, he's at the top." That answer I suppose I can live with. For now.

"You should meet him," Victor says.

"I hope he likes me," she says.

I do not believe her.

SEBASTIAN

2022

I WAIT IN the old childhood bedroom, the same one in which I spent the early hours of the morning debating whether to ask my high school crush to the homecoming dance. I slept on the decision, and when I awoke, the orange glare of the sun lit up the bureau and nightstand with a gleam signaling any decision would be consequential, including no decision. Finally picked up the phone to call her even though I already felt the "no" piercing from the other side of the line. The drip in my throat was palpable; you would have thought I was calling to confess a bank robbery. Like to think these were the days before caller-ID, since I hung up before anyone answered, though sadly, pre-caller-ID time was long past.

A knock at the door: a signal rather than a request; it opens without my acknowledgment. She looks at me in an inspecting way I'm not used to. Her eyes reveal a hesitancy, the kind only reserved for errands against one's better judgment. Find myself looking at the way her dark jeans hug her thighs, her silky black hair packed tightly in a ponytail. She keeps her chin elevated just a little toward the ceiling, creating a dignified air I rarely see on someone my own age; then I remember Mother told me the girl's older—can't be that much older.

"Hello, Sebastian," she says after glancing around the room at my *Star Wars* prequel posters. I want warmth. I shouldn't. What I should be is careful. "I had a nice talk with your parents," she says. She sees the plays in my bookcase, silently judging or approving—I can't tell. "This is your childhood room I take it."

I nod. There's never been a girl in here. Heart races. Her hand brushes over the wooden bureau. "Do you know why I'm here, Sebastian?" Don't appreciate the way she addresses me by name. Power move.

"You're here to meet me."

"A lot of men do what you just did. When you do it, you seem like a boy."

"What did I do?" Want to walk up and pinch her armpit, squeeze the flesh 'til she shrieks, 'til I achieve a flash of recognition because I am not a boy, and she will know it. Instead, I try my best to stay with her line of thought, parry whatever she aspires to do to me. "My parents initiated a match," I say.

"A potential match." She assesses my body for the second time in less than two minutes. "You don't like it?"

"What, the match?"

"Me staring at you."

"It's okay."

She grins. "You're not supposed to like it."

"Maybe I do."

"You're lying." Her confidence, which at first is a strange serpent slithering under my skin, becomes familiar now, yet no less threatening; more treacherous because it's harder to see. "Your parents said you were a teacher," she says.

"Permanent substitute teacher."

"Do you want to be a real teacher?"

"We'll see... It's Alabaster."

"Yeah, I went there."

"Why didn't I see you?"

"I'm a little older. Saw you in that musical."

"*Guys and Dolls*?"

She nods. "We spoke for a minute afterwards."

"That's right." I can't remember.

"Can I sit down?"

I clear my clothes off the desk chair. Once she sits, she spins, gazing from the door to the bed and back to me. "My ex also lived with his parents after college."

"Your ex-husband?"

"Boyfriend."

I notice how smooth her face is. Also notice it's a little weird to refer to a former boyfriend as an ex. "Did he live with his parents when you were together?"

"God no."

Feel like I should defend myself, but all I can come up with is... "It's pretty convenient."

"I'm sure it is."

"What did he do when he lived with his parents?"

"He went to med school?"

"Is he a doctor?"

"I don't know what he is now. He was when we were together." She looks at me like I'm holding the answer to some important question, but she's unsure what the question is. "You like being a teacher?" she asks, though I doubt she'd ask a doctor the same thing.

"Sure."

"That's not enthusiastic."

"I'm new at it," I say. "It's different than being the full-time teacher."

"Has anyone showed you how to do it?"

"A few teachers are helping me."

"So you're undecided if you like it?"

"I require more evidence... What do you require?"

"Me?" she says, a bit taken aback.

I nod, displaying my most playful smile.

"You know why I'm here, don't you?" she says.

"You're in The Society."

"Not supposed to say it out loud."

"Oops."

"I am a part of The Society. I woke up last Thursday, and do you know what my first thought was?"

"I better not guess."

"Realized it was time for me to get married."

"Ah."

"That's what I told your parents."

"What did they say?"

"Your mother thought you'd make a good husband."

"That's promising."

"When you are my age. Your mother was sure to clarify that point. I'm Addison, by the way." We shake hands: Addison on my desk chair and me on the bed. Her forthrightness casts an uneasy shadow, making me want to retreat from everything she says. Then I see a vulnerability unearth itself.

"So you concern my mom?"

"Probably."

"That makes two of us."

"Your father is more open to the possibility."

"That's because he doesn't care."

"I doubt that's true."

"Trust me." My eyes return to her legs, still looking taut in those form-fitting black jeans. "Why me?" I ask.

"I saw you on stage one other time—six months ago."

"In *Midsummer's Night's Dream*?"

She nods.

"Did you like my Kentucky accent?"

"Yours was okay. Everyone else's was dismal."

"Thanks." Once I admit to myself she's more mature than I am, everything becomes easier. "Do you plan to date someone first? Before you get married?"

"You're not the only option."

"Didn't say I was."

"I'm making it clear."

"Cool; I don't know if I'm ready to get married."

She relaxes her posture in the chair. "But you're ready to date?"

"Well, yeah." Shouldn't have come off so eager. I wonder how much older she is. She's obviously older. No lines protruding underneath her eyelids, but her face is detailed in a more permanent way. "You don't know me."

Addison moves forward in her chair; I can smell her grapefruit breath. "You're right—I don't." She shrugs. "You're lucky I want to do this."

CARSON

2022

LOS ANGELES HAS a way of sneaking up on its inhabitants. When you first arrive, the West Side palm trees and traffic and smog descend on the senses. They violate one's view of what it means to thrive with grace. The purr of a deal initiated, deals you're not a part of, create a cocoon of longing, a hyperbolic, ever-constant lament. You see the movers and the shakers, eating salmon Benedicts on their semiprivate verandas, just out of reach. You drive the same highways, munch on the same vegan burgers. You smell the same ocean. You want to be a part of whatever it is that churns the city, that unidentifiable entity that brought you here in the first place. And so the blind spots begin to seem slight, part of the scenery, a particular type of sand on the beach—grainy. You begin to mimic overheard conversations along the promenade, ones that allow you to position yourself among the aspirational chatter. It doesn't matter if your proposals, heard by few, in the end, amount to nothing. Just the fact that you envisioned them makes them more real for yourself. That visualization is enough to get you to the next lunch, the next meet-up, the next time you place yourself among the movers and shakers even though your contribution to the cultural conversation amounts to absolutely nothing.

The moments of doubt maim the skin like the innocent-looking tree bark you scrape against while not paying attention. Once the first cut materializes, you begin to scratch; the irritation spreads without end. One solution to the periodic paranoia is to pretend you've already made it: the breakthrough's occurred—rest easy, you tell yourself: you're simply waiting for the imaginary paycheck to clear. I begin to research condos on the West Side. I can make the purchase as soon as Paolan and I sell the screenplay. I go so far as to weigh the advantages of purchasing a one-bedroom versus a two-bedroom—the differences between living in Brentwood and Silver Lake. Check the bank account: notice how funds evaporate into the ether when one does not cash a regular paycheck. Yet, if one subscribes to already believing the breakthrough's occurred, then the little detail of when the payment will arrive is negligible. I stop reading scripts for Paolan. His failure to pay me for the majority of coverage I write only confirms the production company—despite its shiny logo and the grand estate of its CEO—is less a production company and more a criminal enterprise dressed in sanguine trappings.

Because I could not secure any other internship, and my college friends have become more reclusive, I try to connect with Paolan—foster some kind of nascent friendship. He keeps his distance. As I near the end of the screenplay draft, he takes longer and longer to respond to my texts. I become disheartened by the likelihood that Paolan will dislike the script, or worse, revise it on his own. If he wanted to write it, he should have attempted a draft before pitching the premise to me. The guy never even wrote an outline.

Paolan's tendency to mention mythical fire-breathing dragons and feral felines even though the world of the script calls for neither highlights just how necessary it is for me to maintain control over the crux of our story. The production company's new offices are located off an empty side street in Westwood, but he's never invited me there. Once in a while, Paolan will call me on the phone with some ideas he has regarding one of the main characters. I suggest meeting him at the new offices. He refuses. "Yah, much easier to relay the suggestions over the phone," he says. I consider stopping by in the middle of the day, but Paolan has made things clear in no uncertain terms. He does not want me inside those offices, causing me to further suspect the company is involved in something criminal. Or they plan to steal the movie out from under me.

The morning I finish the draft, I shoot Paolan a text, broadcasting the good news. I plan to set up a meeting, perhaps in the office space for the first time. I run errands in the afternoon, and when I return home, leave my phone on the coffee table, hoping it's going to buzz, though I'm skeptical. At 10 PM, when I've given up hope for the day, the phone rattles. Upon reading the text, I discover he wants to meet me tonight. Odd. The text is vague on details; he demands that once I arrive, I help him drink all the beer he's ordered for his table.

A gaming and karaoke bar in a run-down shopping mall on the east side of downtown hosts Paolan and a few of his friends along with Natalie, the girl I met at the screening. In order to gain entry to the club, I wander through a dimly-lit parking structure where orange warning cones cut off all admittance to any working elevators and a rotted stairway is the only entryway to the open-air bridge leading to the vacated mall. Truncated 1980s rock anthems lead me to the bar. No one greets me at the entrance: no security nor any supervision exists. Inside, the beat overwhelms hidden loudspeakers, disorienting my trek to the place they're all hiding in. Scents of cherry bubblegum infiltrate my nostrils as I practically march toward the loudest room. Upon entry, azure lights seep down, bestowing patches of illumination upon unsteady heads of intoxicated participants. In between bursts of synthesized beats and ill-advised strobe, I can perceive Paolan's long wavy hair and confident swagger. The blurs of light reveal him dancing to the screeching syncopated melodies. His unsteady swaying betrays his intoxication. No one even notices me at first; they're all too caught up lip syncing words to songs they've likely never heard before. Paolan's movements are boisterous, vaguely threatening. He points at everyone without making eye contact in a weird, orchestrated dance meant to disorient and badger. If this person had shown up at the interview, I would have never accepted his internship/screenwriting jobs in the first place. Michael, the second employee of the production company, is there, dumping beer on his head between swigs. The commotion is so on another level. Difficult to believe it's only five inebriated South Africans.

Natalie's the first one to notice my entry. When she nods at me, it's clear she hasn't consumed nearly as much alcohol as the others. I move toward her, brushing loose confetti and streamers out of the way. She meets me at the main table away from Paolan and his fans, who ascend the makeshift stage, lost in bellicose revelry.

"You came," she says, fairly pleased.

"I was invited at the last minute. Where did you guys find this place?"

"Some poster attached to a tree from like ten years ago, right? It's right up Paolan's alley."

"Is it?"

"He likes to feel like he's disappeared."

"Mission accomplished."

She's pleased, but it's a business smile. "Did you do the coverage for the Alchalai script?"

I nod, trying to remember a single detail about the story in the midst of the karaoke turmoil. It was one of the last ones I read for them.

"We liked it—your coverage. The script was just okay, right?"

"But you're making the film?"

"If it were up to me—no way. It's not up to me. Then again, the film only needs a smallish budget."

"Isn't the script written for a strong male and female lead?"

"All the more reason to introduce some fresh faces."

This was code for crazy small budget. If they ever chose to film it, the haphazard script would doom the production. The movie would never see a theater. Paolan's stylized pointing gesture finally shifts to my direction: I'm spotted. He bends his forefinger and middle finger toward me. I approach the stage. After slapping me hard on the back, he tells me to meet him at his table in five minutes. Apparently there are more '80s song lyrics to butcher, so I wait for him, wondering why he wanted me to join him in his respite from reality.

I can smell the sweat when he finally sits across from me. His eyes are bloodshot; he breathes through his mouth, which creates a more imposing demeanor than I'm used to seeing him embody.

"Where's the script, Carson?"

"I sent it to you this morning."

He takes a swig of beer. "Yah, but where's the *script*?"

"I don't understand."

"Yah, you do."

I look at him; he's still waiting for me to say something he'll like. Instead, I ask a question I'm afraid to pose. "You read it?"

He smiles. "Yah, I read it. Where's the script, buddy?"

I look at him blankly.

"Grab yourself a beer," he says. Natalie watches us from a safe distance. She's no doubt afraid to intervene in whatever Paolan's begun, the bar an excuse to unleash rage he no doubt suffers from living the life of a true philistine. Who hires someone to write a script from their own idea?

"You don't like my vision?" I ask.

"Your vision?" he says with annoyance. "That's good."

"I created the characters' names, their personalities. You gave me an idea. I wrote everything from the ground up."

"Keep telling yourself that, buddy." He lifts his chin, gaining the thinnest of elevations on me, like he's looking down from some hillside when in actuality it's mere inches. "There's a lot you can learn. You'll see once I finish my draft."

"I thought you were giving me notes."

He shakes his head and turns to watch one of his colleagues sway drunkenly to a Def Leppard groove.

"You don't know what makes green in this town, buddy," he mumbles under his breath. He leans back in his chair, satisfied. I see it now: his plan was to hold a solid first draft in his hand so he could turn around and make cosmetic changes. In the end, he'd claim the whole piece for himself.

"You going to develop the film at the production company?" I ask.

"I don't think my film is the right fit."

"Your film?" I say incredulously.

"Got a handful of producers I want to show it to."

"Once you make your changes."

"Yah." He grins, the arrogance of his family wealth evoking a flicker in his eyes. There's something sour about the whole scene unfolding. All the movies I grew up watching years ago—*Gladiator, Minority Report, There Will be Blood*—the worlds of those films were larger than what seemed attainable. That they arose from the imaginations of writers and filmmakers made me want to create my own worlds, and hopefully, audience members would get to live in those worlds for two hours a pop someday. Yet guys like Paolan hold the keys even if they're as new to the town as me. The business is a monstrous mountain, spanning a terrain wider than anyone would expect; the only way to scale the massive thing is through others' generosity and risk, two qualities no one seems to personify. Foolish to ever consider Paolan a partner; he is and always will be for Paolan—he will continue to provide himself with the industrious appearance of unearned accomplishment. He's not imagining deals—he's making them, even if they go nowhere. He's able to leverage his connections again and again. I'll need to leave once my money runs out. Paolan will still be here.

The dream, always off in the distance, always spurring me on because of its enormity requires nothing less than my entire commitment. Its sheer implausibility only becomes plausible through my optimism and borderline delusion. The scent of the delusion, the salty Pacific, bouncing off the cliffs of Malibu at dusk, now turns to fermented machismo blended with used candy wrappers and painted-over vanilla walls of run-down karaoke. As I realize there are few cards left to play, a rage passes through my gut. I feel it traveling up my lungs. Paolan watches, content with the dominance he's exhibited. He's about to dismiss me from the room, from the partnership, but rage is on the move.

When people let you know they can take advantage of you with impunity, you want to tell them they can't. That they actually can is irrelevant. But tonight, in the abandoned shopping mall, on the edge of the city of dreams, something shifts in the atmosphere—something empowering, and it's not the ability to secure a lawyer within forty-eight hours, which I will do in due time. My right hand stretches toward Paolan like I'm grasping for something indiscernible. I'm pushing him away, yet drawing him in. He doesn't see any of it.

It takes a moment for him to realize something's occurring, and in the interim, he grins without a trace of avarice. He still holds complete control of the hollowed-out room, but things are shifting. His selfishness is an effect necessary for survival. His unwillingness to connect is part of his upbringing. I can sense it somehow. He's only doing what he's been taught by the family back home. We both know he's made conscious choices and greatly benefited from them, and in this interim, I see all his choices, seize upon them, twist them like a wet rag so they seem like compounded mistakes. All his choices—everyone he's screwed over—cross my subconscious. I can see their faces—their forlorn eyes and trusting stares. Whatever it is I'm about to wrestle control of is forbidden. It's the raw emotion we're repeatedly told to avoid, the violet summoning of rage. The mindset brings on cancer if you flirt with it too often. But somehow, I've found a way to avoid harming myself, and in the process, the rage becomes a weapon.

I see his father holding his hand as they stare up at an out-of-focus Table Mountain in Cape Town. The dazzling sunrise temporarily blinds their vision.

"We're going to climb the thing," his father says. "I want to see the top of Lion's Head Summit."

"I can't even see the top," the boy says.

The father looks up at the immense scale of the cliffs, how they shadow the city like a spiderweb. "Why do you need to?" he asks his son.

"How will we even do it?"

The father gives the boy a push. "We start moving."

"I don't want to."

"It isn't your decision."

"Why don't you act like Mother?" the boy asks.

"She's weak." He grips the boy's shirt tighter. "Do you want to be weak?"

"No!"

"Yah, but you are." He grabs hold of the boy's hand and begins to drag him through the golden sand. The boy makes the only play he has left. He collapses to the ground in a fit of rage. His knees dig into the earth with gusto, leaving an imprint not just in the sand, but in his memory, where he'll bury this moment. The child will be unable to deal with the disappointment he knows he's brought to his father. The child's feeling of vulnerability and eventual emotional abandonment will need to be replaced with something more attuned to everyday survival, something central to human persuasion, not dissimilar to what the father currently wields against the boy.

I stand next to that same boy, now a man, whose tears now scatter and dissolve. The adult Paolan stands by my side, transfixed by the boy's facial expression of loss. Nothing need be said. He knows he's the boy. He's forgotten it all until this second.

"What are you doing?" the adult Paolan manages to ask as he looks away toward the mountain even though we're still in the karaoke room.

Did I summon all this or was it simply a wave I managed to catch? I do not afford him an answer, nor myself. With a turn of my head, we're back in the karaoke club, sweating a storm of '80s songs. I grip the barstool I'm sitting on for balance. Paolan gazes at me, unsure what to say or how to process what he's seen. Does he remember what I've shown him? I look beyond his eyes, behind the pupils, and see the trepidation residing underneath—first time for him. He still remembers.

I look at my clammy hands. What did I just do?

MOIRA

2010

VICTOR DOESN'T WANT to know what the boys are capable of. As his own powers diminish, he works to rid himself of the trappings and advantages The Society offers. Meanwhile, my own abilities swell, unbeknownst to Victor. A normalizing phenomenon occasionally manifests itself among our members; Victor never believes it could happen to him. He believes, or so he tells himself, that a withdrawal from The Society would benefit our family in the long run. I happen to disagree with that assessment. When the boys turn seven, I want to know what abilities, if any, are locked away deep inside them, waiting to emerge at the right time.

In most cases, the right time requires asserting oneself. The first time I was able to access anything was in the middle of Raymond's communication with the child ghost. I wanted to see what Raymond did. My desire to match his ability spurred me to action. Unfortunately, to get a child to assert themselves, they really must be threatened. Accessing an ability would require a child to be wronged in some manner.

When the boys are ten, Raymond suspects that out of two children, one must be carrying the ability. Accessing the necessary emotion will require a jolt to the senses, and for a child, the jolt must be raw, their world under threat—perhaps even the element of surprise must be used against them. I refuse Raymond's wishes, will not allow my boys to feel that they need to run, especially if they are too young to really know how. "We are all tested, at one time or another," he reassures me.

"Not me."

"That was your parents' doing."

"They wanted to protect me," I insist.

"From what?"

I glare at him. "You."

"Your children will be far more protected if we know." His use of the "we" should alert me. It doesn't.

I still refuse, but then he promises to do things in a way that will boost their adrenaline without making them think they're in danger.

On a night when the moon forms a crescent and Victor is still at work, I make my move. Victor has no idea I still carry any association with Raymond. I open the door of the boys' bedroom. My hands brush across each of their warm beds. Whisper for them to follow me. Sebastian is slow to rouse, but Carson's transition from deep sleep to sharpness surprises me. Both boys find their coats without fuss.

Raymond tells me the boys will race. The exertion will bring about the necessary agitation. When the boys and I reach the field at the edge of Jefferson Parish, Raymond is not there to meet us. I feel the push from him—subtle, but it is there. Leave the boys for a moment: an indifferent Sebastian and Carson wait impatiently; their initial enthusiasm fades by the second. They want to go back to sleep.

Underneath the moonlit silhouette of a conifer, Raymond appears, revealing his real plans to me, the ones he no doubt holds from the start. "We'll leave them here," he says.

"What do you mean?"

He stares off down the field with a cool vacantness. "They need to feel lost. Temporarily abandoned."

"Forget it."

He places his hand on my arm. The pressure is palpable. "It's okay, Moira."

"You don't have children. Like Malcom."

"What?"

"It's from *Macbeth*."

He does a poor job of masking his impatience with me. "I never read that. It will only be for a half-hour."

"Absolutely not."

"Would you rather they run instead?"

"What do you mean?"

He lurches forward and knocks me down, taking off in a sprint toward the twins. My view from the ground reveals a man whose precise movements suggest a purpose other than what he purported. His black boots scuff the grass, leaving rough streaks in the earth. He could overtake them if he wanted to; his slower speed betrays his doubt at what he's begun. My hopes he'll stop are dashed when the first jolt of brilliant blue flies out of his right hand, striking a haystack ten feet from the boys, indigo and turquoise ricocheting in a blare of chaos. Luckily, he toys with a lower measurement, not enough to start a fire.

Carson starts running. He stops when he realizes

Sebastian isn't behind him. It takes Sebastian longer to process danger. Once he finally understands, his aggressive nature takes over; the sense of competition engulfs him fully. Sebastian's natural athletic ability allows him to catch up with his brother. The boys head for a small clearing, which leads to a vast swamp. By now, I am back on my feet, in fast pursuit of Raymond, unsure how to stop him without an outright attack.

The second jolt of blue light leaves Raymond's hand and strikes the ground behind where Sebastian's shoes were a moment earlier. Carson stops in his tracks while Sebastian continues to run. Carson regards Raymond running toward him, this strange middle-aged man with surprising boundless energy. All three of their shadows, illuminated by the moonlight, disappear behind the brush.

How to signal Carson to protect his brother before perhaps more severe panic sets in? I stand under a palm meadow, realizing Carson must know I have something to do with this chase, that his mother who should always protect him from danger has somehow placed her two children in peril. Am almost afraid to meet his eyes. I follow them into the brush.

Maybe he doesn't suspect me. Maybe he thinks this strange man is a lone actor, out to get the two of them in the dead of night. Carson, unconcerned with a motive, traverses the swamp, overtaking Sebastian with ease. Never seen Carson run so fast. Believe Raymond will be unable to catch up with them until Sebastian trips on a fallen branch. He takes a tumble, the bark tearing through his blue jeans like an unexpected gash from cutlery. Carson halts, hearing Sebastian's moans echoing through the hollow swamp.

Sebastian looks up at his brother, vulnerable and confused. The blood drips down his leg.

Raymond transitions from a run to a confident stride as he approaches them.

Sebastian, whose overconfidence is thoroughly eradicated, regards Raymond with sheer bafflement.

Raymond grins at my scared little boy, stopping ten feet from him. "Strike me," he tells Sebastian.

Sebastian gazes up at Raymond like he speaks a foreign language. He looks down at his bleeding leg. "With what?"

"I did that to you. Now, defend yourself," Raymond reiterates.

"I don't know how," Sebastian says.

Raymond puts on his sympathetic face. "Instinct."

Sebastian strains his neck to catch Carson's glance.

"Stay away from him," Raymond warns Carson. "It's not your turn."

Carson notices me first. No sounds, no defensive attack from me. A rescue is not underway. His expression says it all. In his line of sight, I am a different entity for the first time. I am part of this, their exposure to real danger my doing.

Raymond, aware of my presence, switches his attention to Carson. "What are you looking at her for?"

"Why wouldn't I look at her? She's my mother."

"I'm the one you should focus on."

Carson frowns. "Don't worry. I'm looking at you too." He nods at Sebastian without taking his attention off Raymond. "Why don't you step back from my brother."

"The boy only needs to defend himself."

Instinctively, Carson replies, "He doesn't know how."

"And you do?"

"I might."

"I want to see."

"I know you do."

Sebastian looks up at Raymond, and seeing Raymond's gaze fix on Carson, he summons some hidden strength and attempts a running charge at Raymond.

I yell for Sebastian to stop, but he doesn't hear me.

"Watch this," Sebastian cries as he hurdles toward Raymond.

Raymond waves his right hand at Sebastian, knocking the wind right out of him mid-run. Raymond calls out to me, the disappointment sneaking into his voice. "He doesn't have it."

Carson watches for my response, for further confirmation that I do in fact know this strange man.

"So he doesn't," I answer matter-of-factly. "Now, leave him alone."

Carson regards his brother, lying unconscious on the grass. "What did you do to him?" he screams at Raymond.

Raymond, pleased he no doubt has jump-started Carson's anger, smiles at my boy. "Pretty upset, I see."

Carson glares at him. "Help him."

Raymond gestures for Carson to proceed closer. "You help him."

Carson takes a few steps toward Sebastian, watching to see if Raymond will try to stop him. When it appears he has a clear path, Carson advances, only to be slammed by a gust of air that Carson likely suspects comes from the ether. It doesn't. Carson wipes his mouth and pickes himself up from the cold ground.

Raymond smiles. "Push me back."

"Step away from my brother."

"I will if you push me."

Carson tries to catch my gaze. I lock eyes with him, urging him on.

"Believe me, I want to," Carson says.

"Then do it." Raymond allows him more time before realizing a particular element is missing from his scheme. "You do understand I know your mother."

"Seems that way."

"Want to know how?"

"I'll pass."

"Or are you afraid? Let me help you." Raymond approaches him.

Carson steps back as Raymond advances.

I run toward Sebastian. I've had just about enough of Raymond toying with my sons. Carson sees me approach first. He appears relieved and hurt at the same time.

Raymond keeps his eyes on Carson. "Let me handle this, Moira."

Carson flinches at the sound of my name slipping off Raymond's lips. It is as if I have orchestrated the entire exercise—and in a way, I have.

Carson closes his eyes and reaches toward Raymond, causing Raymond to stop in his tracks. Raymond grimaces, bracing himself for some unknown hurdle about to plummet his way. Even though it's what he wants, I can detect a scintilla of alarm.

Raymond stands in place awaiting the onslaught like a parent in the passenger seat during a driving lesson. I imagine he expects a push, a gust of wind perhaps, but after thirty seconds, it's evident Carson is poking in an unfamiliar realm, just like his mother.

Indeterminate sounds sweep out of Carson before he forms the words to speak. "Who are you?" he asks as he continues to probe.

Raymond attempts his best efforts to appear nonplussed.

I gather Sebastian in my arms. He looks up at Carson, unsure what is transpiring.

Damp air clings to my neck, leaving a tingle of pinpricks.

Carson closes his eyes. "What's The Society?" he says.

Raymond's lips form into a smirk. "Good."

"You've talked to ghosts?"

"Occupational hazard," Raymond says.

"What am I doing?" Carson's eyes are closed. He looks like he's skimming a message whose words are too small to read.

"That's quite enough," Raymond says.

Carson smiles, stretching his hand out further. "You are my age, walking off a train. You feel an itch creep through your boots, your toes, the wetness difficult to shake. You're a little sad, leaving a train full of strangers for a city full of strangers. But you do it because someone told you you'd be great if you managed to leave your home behind. It's harder than you thought, and you know it."

Raymond glares at Carson. "Put your hand down, kid."

I am within striking distance, and Raymond sees.

"Don't come any closer, Moira."

"You said it would only be a test."

"More than that now."

"He's only a boy."

"That's what concerns me."

While Carson watches our conversation play out in real time, he lets his guard down.

Raymond leans in to attack, but I dispatch him to the ground with a wave of my hand.

Stunned at first, Raymond eases off the clammy leaves as he wipes the sweat from his brow.

Carson looks at me in awe.

"By tomorrow morning," Raymond says, "neither of them will remember any of this."

ADDISON

2022

MY PARENTS ARE dupes. I don't hold it against them. Not their fault; they cannot help their inadequacies, though I wish they'd try harder to compensate. I wish they would match the moment they were born to, the potential they should have harnessed. I do not begrudge them for lacking the ability: their failure to manipulate their surroundings is happenstance, not their own shortcoming. But I wish my parents had guided me. They simply lacked the will to plunge into the arena. When the ability skips a generation, the offspring are left to decipher the mysteries and the burdens. Our birthright is larger than the legacy our parents leave us.

The marriage—or should I say "the establishment of the relationship"—is my Uncle Raymond's idea. He is the one with the ability, a substantial one, and the wherewithal to use it. It's the reason he's in charge. A few times he's taken me on his rounds: the expensive service he provides for those seeking the afterlife. It's peculiar to see him in that role, attending to those in such dire need of some kind of reassurance, projecting some acknowledged understanding that things will be better than they are now. His true capacity for empathy is suspect, but he puts on a good show.

He tells me to meet him for coffee one morning in the Quarter, a week after I meet Sebastian. I make my way down St. Ann's, wondering if Uncle will sneak up on me, which he does from time to time. He must think it's endearing, some type of jolly affectation I'm supposed cherish as his niece. I hate it. In fact, I think it's weak, these little surprises of his. For someone who prides himself on disengaging for the sake of instilling unease, he seems determined at times to seek my approval. But maybe not today.

The humidity is dense with bitter scents of expired alcohol and left-out garbage. I regret the flip-flops and airy spaghetti strap top I'm sporting; I should have spruced myself for the meeting. Shops and restaurants do not open as early as they used to. The city is still in partial recovery mode from the most recent hurricane, which struck Jefferson Parish head-on. The flooding waded inside the pores of Orleans Parish. The first hurricane at the beginning of the century nearly destroyed the city. I was old enough to process the devastation, but they whisked us away to safety. We looked on from afar as the water strangled the city's poorer inhabitants, washing their homes away. In my child's mind, I envied them a little, wishing to commiserate in the city's shared struggle. Yet, when my own generation's hurricane came, I sought to ignore the lasting implications as best I could.

The antique wooden door squeaks as it opens; the ceiling fans blow circulated warm air, which tickles my skin. I wipe the condensation from my arm and ignore the college-age males checking me out—they're not much younger, but I pretend the age difference is sizable. The sparse lighting conceals the facial expressions of the patrons. The café might as well be hidden in another realm. Uncle probably loves it.

Unfortunately, he's already sitting in the back on an iron bench, comfortable in his position of strength, which allows him to see the entire room. He looks older than the last time I saw him. Shouldn't be surprised—after all, he *is* old. Or at least older than Mother and Father. He could be my great-uncle. His jowls are pronounced. His glance—still probing, but now holds the slightest glint. His chin rests on his fist; he's been looking at me since I entered and only turns away when I meet his gaze, his embarrassed grimace a lone afterthought.

I slide onto the bench opposite him. He pushes the pitcher of water toward me without saying a word.

"Pour yourself a glass," he says. Uncle likes to give directions at the start of conversations to express control.

"Hello, Uncle," I say as I begin to pour.

He looks me over, no doubt disapproving of my flimsy top. I begin counting how long we will go before he asks about Sebastian. "What did you think of him?" he asks. Not long, apparently. A slippery smile sneaks out his lips. He knows my response is hardly the final matter on the subject.

"He's confident," I say.

"I've heard that," he says.

I grin. "Suppose that's a good thing."

"Naturally."

I take a sip of water, attempting to lighten my forthcoming criticism. "I'm not sure how smart he is."

"Intelligence is rarely an easy trait to discern."

"Isn't it though?"

"There's different types," he says.

"Think that's a cop-out."

He smiles. "Maybe. Don't be too quick to judge. It's a hell of a match."

"Because of his mother."

Uncle looks away, then nods.

It's always difficult to tell how comfortable I can be in front of him. "I can sense her," I say. "Is she a threat to you?"

"His mother? Addison, everyone is some type of threat. That doesn't mean we do not live."

I dig further. "You know her though."

"Are you asking me how *well* I know her?"

"I suppose."

He stretches his torso across the bench. "None of your business."

I begin to think Uncle has hoisted Sebastian on me for his own benefit. Why I didn't see that from the start is my own fault. "He has no ability," I say with finality.

"That's why you're safe with him."

I can feel my temperature rise. "Why do I need to be safe?"

"Really want to be with someone who might jeopardize your leadership?"

"I'm too young to think about that now."

Uncle's teeth are a white painted fence, shielding me from his true feelings on the subject.

"He has a brother," I say.

Uncle's expression changes, a little concern slipping through. "He's in Los Angeles." He makes an exaggerated gesture with his arms. "The film business."

"He has the ability, doesn't he? I think I sensed him when he was in high school."

Uncle studies the wall alongside us. "Not when he's away from the city."

"What makes you think he won't come back?"

"He won't. Don't you worry."

SEBASTIAN

2022

I AVOID CHATTING with other faculty members and bring my lunch back to the empty auditorium—lots of sketch planning to lay out. Also percolating ideas for a spring play in case they hire me for that. Wentworth's voice bellows across the rafters.

"I remember when you and your brother were in the musical. You remember that?"

I spin around: how did he enter without me seeing? "Of course I do; I think about that show a lot."

Wentworth nods thoughtfully. "I'm sure. You both brought down the house."

"It was the highlight of my time here. When we were the two gangsters in *Kiss Me Kate*."

"What was the name of that number of yours?"

"Brush Up Your Shakespeare."

Wentworth's eyes glimmer. "Yes! I loved that song."

"We tipped our hats at the end of our musical number as we strolled up the aisle. The crowd went wild."

"Sure would be nice to return to that moment."

"What do you mean?"

"You should get up on stage. Stroll through the house again."

"Why?"

"Sit down, Sebastian."

I sit a few house seats away from him. I face Wentworth at an awkward angle.

"It's not every day I receive a call from four different parents," he says. "Upset their kids can't participate in their own club."

"What?"

"You only invited one student to come up on stage on the first day of improv."

"I was showing them how it's done."

"They didn't stop by to watch you act."

"Are you serious?"

"Of course I'm serious."

"The audience shouted out different scenarios."

"That's not good enough."

"I can't believe they complained. They told me it was great!"

"If you want to become a teacher, Carson, you're going to need to go to grad school. We don't have room here for the learning curve you require."

"I'm only a substitute teacher."

"I can't weather the risk you bring with you."

"Please give me a chance."

"I did; you're done."

If there had been a fence outside the school, I would have jumped it. The pungent scent of the oak trees infiltrates my lungs as my feet thump against the sidewalk pavement. I run farther and farther away from my car. The bridge to my adult life, admittedly a shortcut, eradicated in an instant. Can feel my grievances already forming. The disorientation almost hurts. I was making a difference with the younger folk—couldn't he see that? That place was stuffy with poor comedic timing before I showed up. No job to claim to Addison now. Panic on the move.

One time in middle school, I had a panic attack at the Riverwalk. So many people swarming through the food court like angry bees. My sense of equilibrium was truncated. Joints completely froze outside TCBY yogurt. It was the first time I had been anywhere without my parents. Even though Carson was twenty feet away, it didn't seem to matter. Breath shortened; the panic crept in. It was as if someone dropped an anvil on each foot— the imagined pain ignited my tears, which didn't cease once they began flowing. Unfortunately for me, there were two other boys with us; both saw my sniffles and proceeded to point. Carson arrived on the scene and calmed me down. Once the panic subsided, my new worry amounted to what these guys would say on Monday—would they tell the other guys? The girls? I imagined future shame and began to concoct some excuse of a story in case the guys outed my cowardness.

I decide to stop at the streetcar tracks and catch my breath. Drops of moisture drip from my forehead onto my chin. It's startling how many options I present myself with. The first and most appealing: I'll pretend to work at school until I can figure out what to do next. I like this option because it keeps Addison off my back. My job was the whole reason Father and Mom were able to settle the match—can't let that fall apart. Option two: tell Addison I'm no longer employed there, but for option two to be viable, I'm going to need another means of employment. The streetcar *ding* sounds, and as it approaches, I decide to take a little ride. It's unlikely I would leave with five months left of the school year, so whatever new job I "choose," it must be something I can claim as part-time before the school year ends. My legs ache as I board the streetcar; the unsettled nature of what's in front of me flows through my joints. Nevertheless, not many chances to lean back in your seat and watch the slow drizzle of life scroll by when you're working every afternoon. The crisp sound of a seven-iron smacking a golf ball down a fairway can be heard in the distance. We have a golf course here? Since when? A sudden urge arises to walk along a fairway, the prickly green trim cushioning my shoes. Then I remember the time Father took Carson and me to Audubon Golf Course, a snappy little par-3 among the sprawling oak trees and violets.

SEBASTIAN

2013

IT IS A particularly stifling summer; you step out the front door into a sauna. Makes a shower almost pointless, though Mom begs to differ. Carson sits indoors reading thick books—fiction I think. Don't bother to scrutinize the covers when he isn't in his room, like I did when we were younger. While Carson reads the day away, I brave the overgrown grass of our condensed backyard. Had cut my own little fringe just before my makeshift putting green. Cock my wrists, snap the ball with my sand wedge so the ball shoots up at a vertical angle, easing itself down with the patience of a loving parent upon my homemade green. Swing is okay, but Carson's is dreadful. No competition there because Carson takes zero interest in the game while I busy myself discovering the solitary beauty of being left with your thoughts while your gaze focuses on a bright yellow ball.

So I am surprised to say the least when Father takes Carson and me to Audubon and begins to lecture us, as if we have both picked up a seven-iron for the very first time. My defense mechanisms kick in. Father's guidance frustrates me on two fronts. One, he takes no notice of my prior efforts to practice and excel on my own, right in our backyard. He also assumes without any evidence that Carson and I are on equal footing in the impromptu competition he creates between us two brothers.

Yet it's kind of touching to see Father try to dispel his limited wisdom on the game of golf to both his sons: one who could care less, and the other—let's be honest—who has already surpassed Father's own overall skill level, even though he can still outdrive me. When the spikes of my golf shoes sink into the dirt and my left eye glances out toward the finite fairway ahead, I hear Father whispering to Carson, his true purpose revealing itself. He wants the tee box, the fairways, and Carson's 8-iron to assess Carson's otherworldly abilities—not his golf swing. I crack the ball straight down the line; try to pretend my guess about Father's motives isn't at all true as I make a self-satisfied gesture. Carson slices one into the oak trees. Father approaches, dropping a red Titleist ball at Carson's feet.

"Try it again," Father says.

"Why?" Carson asks.

"Just do it, but this time, close your eyes."

"How am I going to hit the ball if I can't see the thing?"

"Just *do* it," he reiterates.

My own ball is yards ahead, one more shot to the green, but when Carson shanks the ball on his second attempt and Father drops yet another ball in front of my brother, my achievement fades like September sunshine.

"Hey, are we going to play?" I call out.

"Hold on, Sebastian," Father says.

I nod, disgusted. I want to take my club and hurl it

past the tee box, or better yet, at both of them.

"Just humor him," Carson mumbles. His attempts do nothing to quiet my resentment.

"You humor him," I murmur. "I just want to play my lie."

Father brushes me off with a dismissive gesture. "In a minute." He places another ball on Carson's tee. "This time I want you to slow things down."

"You want me to hit in slow motion?" Carson asks.

"No, I want you to slow things down."

"That's not the same thing?"

"It's *different*."

I don't stick around to hear Carson's response or give him a chance to try his swing because I leave both of them at the tee box and head out after my ball. If Father wants Carson to hit the ball again, Carson will need to hit me. I wouldn't mind a helmet though.

Carson is unable to outdrive me that afternoon, but he eventually makes contact with his ball on the next hole. What follows disturbs both of us. Just off the green on the third hole, the ball shoots up from under Carson's sand wedge and plops five inches from the pin. Carson smiles the smile of someone whose luck finally manages to surpass his own limited expectations. Father doesn't smile. He marches toward Carson holding another ball in his hand, dropping it at Carson's foot. "Do it again," he says.

To his credit, Carson answers, "No, we're in the middle of a round. It's Sebastian's shot."

"I'm not asking," Father says.

I will later discover Father's own abilities are evaporating, which explains a trace of his obsession with

Carson, yet at the time, I'm incapable of balancing such opposing ideas.

Carson steals a glance at me but neglects to wait for my reaction. He knows who he needs to please.

Father points at the ball. "Think about replicating what you achieved. In every way."

"How do I do that?"

"Visualize exactly what you did from start to finish. Then do it again."

Carson flips his head back, and for a moment, I think he is going to storm off the course. He doesn't. He can't resist the attention and the challenge. He hates golf, and I don't think he yearns for father's approval as much as I do, but Carson's craving to clutch whatever ability resides in the hidden part of himself is too tempting. His knees pivot in the same manner as the prior shot, and even before the ball reaches full velocity, I know it is going to land in the exact same spot. A hideous cracking sound as Carson's ball slaps down on top of his other ball. Neither father nor son make eye contact with each other. This isn't about golf. It is about some gift Carson has that I lack. Whatever I accomplish in the future will pale in comparison to Carson's burgeoning power deep within himself. I decide to play the rest of the round on my own, maintaining a hole ahead of them. Neither bother to protest. I become used to moments like this.

SEBASTIAN

2022

THE STREETCAR HALTS in front of Audubon Course. After the hurricane, the city invested into making the place one of the top public courses in the country. I step off with no clubs and no plan. Only wish to walk towards the pin and remember when I used to be sort of good at something. There's a tame metal fence that borders the rest of the park. You can practically follow along for a bit like you're caddying for some unknown strangers, dispensing imaginary advice to no one in particular. However, any hopes for quiet voyeurism are dashed. The surrounding area is packed; voluntary security in tightly-fitted green polos fan out as best they can. Some tournament I've never heard of is underway. Groups of twosomes line the first tee box, decked out in bright caps with their chosen sponsors. Don't spot any golfers I know, and I do know some. Hustle past the entryway without showing a ticket and continue toward the driving range, hoping to spot a golfer I recognize, someone I can focus on amid the tumult I feel inside. At first, I only see minor golfers, struggling for a paltry piece of the tour, tussling to qualify any way they can. It's tough out there when you decide to do a thing professionally, knowing you'll likely never breach your own goal marker, fumbling a bit outside the line even though you know damn well your performance is objectively stellar—just not quite good enough. That's how I feel about everything. Then I see his shoes. They're the first thing to catch my gaze: black golf cleats with a silver finish—they honestly look more like basketball shoes. He wears a cream polo with turquoise stripes running perpendicularly—black pants and a black cap, but some of his loose blonde hairs escape through the space between the cap and the plastic fastener. He smacks the ball out past the farthest flag. His gathering of groupies try to follow the ball after it leaves their field of vision. It's Skip Mackadoo in the flesh.

Mackadoo made his name by winning every tournament while at Stanford after an impoverished childhood in rural Ireland. Mackadoo and I are the same age. There's something stirring when a person in his early twenties can see the dark tunnel but also glimpse the inviting warm glow of a possible future. Double stirring when they venture through the tunnel without hesitancy or doubt; most people never do.

After his beautiful drive, he shifts his body like a penguin in order to drag another golf ball towards the tee and notices me watching him.

"Hello there," he mumbles from underneath his sunglasses.

"Hey, Mackadoo," I manage to say.

"You a local?"

"Yeah, this is where I'm from." I almost say, "I'm American" but stop myself.

"Well, enjoy this drive." His backswing takes off

before shifting his weight and striking perfectly through the target. The tee flips up into the air, dancing gently above the precisely cut grass. Instead of watching the ball, I keep my eye focused on the tee until it finally flutters to the ground. Another spectator nearby calls out, "Charming."

Mackadoo turns to face me and five others watching him. "I've been working with my 8-iron of late. It is, in fact, the most underrated club."

"Not when you're done with it," I say.

A few laughs. He takes off his cap, brushes his hand through his golden hair, and points to me. "Exactly, young man."

Except again, we're the same age. I wish I knew more about golf. I could start a real conversation, perhaps strike up a friendship. Every so often I'm reminded of the fact I do not have any of those. At least not since Carson left for Los Angeles. My desire for friendship with Mackadoo intertwines with feelings of competition. For me, they're interconnected. I imagine he'll proceed to shoot a mediocre round, which I base on his obvious desire to interact with his little following in contrast to the other golfers around him, who remain as focused as a high school scholar taking the SAT. His girlfriend, a costar on one of those teen dramedies, who tries too hard to appear seventeen even though she's pushing twenty-seven, is probably waiting for him back at the hotel. Try to stay focused on his next shot. He lets his 8-iron fly, but the effort appears too mechanical; it lacks the joyous bounce one would expect from a pro, but the ball does manage to land in a respectable position near the practice pin. He looks back at us again and winks. He really is taken with this impromptu following, which consists of a middle-aged couple with matching salmon-colored golf shorts, an elderly gentleman resting on an oversized golf umbrella like it's some cane, and two younger girls in their early thirties who quietly debate among themselves whether they should begin flirting with Mackadoo.

Once he begins the round, a caddy will carry his bag, occasionally offer a club. But what if another kind of associate followed him around the course? Someone who could dispense the advice he truly yearns for. Like when to pump his fist at the crowd. Granted you need an excellent shot for those, but they're bound to happen in a round even if you're not resting atop the leader board. After two more similar shots, which appear way too mechanical but land near the pin, Mackadoo tosses the 8-iron back in his bag and does his best to smile through what he must know is not a shot a true champion makes. I imagine he's searching for the perfect joke, as if his emotional connection with this respectful little gathering rests on his ability to consistently entertain them. Unfortunately for him, his comedic abilities are limited. But imagine if he retained some kind of entertainment coach in his back pocket? Who knows what endorsements he'd be able to land? Mackadoo nods to his caddy, who I didn't even notice until now; thought he was one of the onlookers—makes sense. He's too dispassionate for fan status. Mackadoo slips his arms through his tan windbreaker and gazes at his little group like he wants them to say the first goodbye.

"Knock 'em dead, Mackadoo," I say.

He beams, relieved for my encouragement. He probably knows he's going to blow the round. "I'll do that, so." He leaves us to watch the back of his polo shirt as a cluster of palm meadows obscure our vision of him. My mind rushes with adrenaline. The same kind of acting advice I could dispense to the kids, I could entrust to Mackadoo.

I sense a kindred spirit in this guy. We could call him The Irishman with the follow-through. We'd hone his performative qualities: gather new crowds ten times the size of today's, and I'd be at the center of it all as Mackadoo's performance coach. Addison would be so impressed. So would Mom and Dad. I'd like to see the look on Carson's face when he sees me standing on television next to a jubilant Mackadoo at Pebble Beach, the wind ripping through our hair, wearing faces of self-righteousness at the adoration we've cultivated on the course and the victory we've achieved due to Mackadoo's increased confidence now that he can wow a crowd—all thanks to me.

ADDISON

2022

LIGHT A LEMON indigo candle. The burning smell never ceases to make me run out of the room for fear of fire. What if conjuring fire were part of my abilities? *Every*one would watch their tone with me.

My natural messiness creates havoc in the apartment. Dirty dishes line the kitchen countertop. I dab some soap in them before I let them sit. Not a cleaning but preparation for leaving them out. Clothes are strewn on the chair, on the floor, on the bed. Sometimes I don't even bother to remove the clothes before I go to sleep. Why pretend to change my cluttered style? It's part of my creativity—better to become an expert at sprucing up the place. Of course, if I lived with someone, they'd find out how disorderly I am.

The hamburger meat crackles on the stove. I fix a salad, sprinkle some pineapple pieces I purchased at Whole Foods. He'll arrive shortly. It's helpful to be cooking when he arrives. Make him feel guilty. Gives him something to work with. Me as well. I've tried starting with approval. With affection. None of it flies.

If you commence with guilt, he has to strive to win you over. He'll feel unsettled in his gut. He'll want to make things right, but he won't be sure how to address it because he didn't do anything to bring the guilt on. He'll think he *must* have done *something*, and that's where you have him. When he approaches you, be kind...don't be stupid. Do not fall into his embrace so easily. You must do so reluctantly. After all, you're busy preparing the meal for the date: for the two of you. He'll feel silly for interrupting your flow at the expense of his selfishness. You may let him rectify his impetuousness if you wish, when you're good and ready.

I am not cold. Not what I want him to think. I am practical. I am busy. I am mature. He may at first regret dating someone six years older than himself. It will not last long. My experience in the arena of life will enhance his own yearning for superiority. I have no doubt.

If I were born into another family...if there was no Society, I might not feel my age. A youthful mindset would stretch into my thirties. New York—maybe Los Angeles. Work at an advertising firm. A life where I can drift. Not this life, which requires a mate and soon. The first attempt in San Francisco ended in failure. I will do what I can, where I can, to learn from my folly.

He is a beautiful creature when I first meet him: sizable pectoral muscles, tight stomach, piercing brown eyes—all helpful attributes to let you know he is on the case. Your scintilla of worry: imperceptible in his eyes. His more advanced age contributes to the allure. He knows his ten-year difference is an advantage, and he wields it gracefully and effectively. Masculinity, the sort I crave, is nearly impossible for a man in his twenties, both physiologically and contextually. While a man in his thirties may appear young with moments of impulsivity and immaturity, standing beside a man in his forties, a man in his thirties is still a man. A man in his twenties, though, is an older boy, attempting to discern how to become a man. Why would a person want that? Why would I? Never mind the fact that I'm twenty-eight.

The man I eventually obtain, my beautiful creature, is also beautifully wounded. His father asks his mother for a divorce because his father cannot handle the stress of being an older boy striving to become a man in his twenties. How prescient. So my beautiful creature makes a concerted effort to be a man as early as possible. His ambitions lead to a medical career. Some suggest taking a year off before medical school: calms the nerves, cleans the slate, he's told. Not my beautiful creature. He doesn't even take a break the summer after school ends, instead opting for an internship at his local hospital so he can immerse himself in blood and urgency. He doesn't care for surprises, though he'd never admit it. Unfortunately, all the preparation in the world cannot prepare you for the unexpected, which awaits each morning you enter the sterile, chalk-white corridors of any ICU.

I meet my beautiful creature not long after he becomes a man. He has already completed his residency and goes on to specialize in cardiology. The grueling pace of his long hours requires he never look up. Patient to patient, procedure to procedure; there is little time for meals or to breathe. He can count on the chaos, and he begins to lean on it, to relish it. The tempo reverberates in his wrists, in his fingers. He has found his calling. The tempo inoculates him to the silent obstacle every doctor must encounter: doubt. Uncertainty lies safely hidden in the recesses of his heart.

And so when he meets me, I sense his self-assurance right away and love it. Cannot get enough. I luxuriously breathe it in before he awakens. He speaks so close to me. Must have stored his affection throughout his long years of medical training. When you store something like that for so long, it unravels in unexpected ways like a perilous tsunami finally making landfall.

Right before I meet my beautiful creature, I leave the Parish after college, not unlike what Sebastian's brother has done. I desire someplace new where I can walk the streets and not know the cracks in the sidewalks by heart, someplace where I am no longer sure when it is about to rain. It has been so long since drops of rain surprise me as they dribble onto my forehead. I want to give up my powers at least for a little while. Wherever I choose needs to resemble the Parish in some respect—I need a semblance of home. Despite my yearning for something novel, if I cannot draw comparisons and carry the essence of the Parish with me, I will literally perish. In San Francisco, when you leave the Wharf on a cloudy day (which is most days), you can step through the gray haze, which sticks to the little hairs on your arm like wet moth balls, and make a seamless jump to an overcast yet welcoming Riverwalk in the Parish. If I can achieve the semblance of the Parish, I will be able to experience the new without the dislocation. It is one thing to temporarily give up powers; it is another to lose my sense of home.

I am at an Italian place not far from the Wharf with a new friend I made at the PR firm. We are munching on breadsticks when some hardened grain gets caught in her throat. She embarks on a choking spell. My eyes dart from table to table in search of a man, I'm sorry to say, someone who looks like they know what it means to take action. Had we been in the Parish, I could have dislodged the grain with a stare and a brush of my hand. The sounds of my friend gasping for air reverberate through the restaurant. My soon-to-be beautiful creature hears the danger and arrives at our table. He wears an untucked white button-down with the sleeves rolled up. Carries himself like a suave senator.

"Do you know CPR?" I ask. I didn't know myself but should have.

He doesn't answer: only a brief moment of acknowledgment. He rolls his sleeves up further and begins to administer it. I watch the life drain from my friend. Silently curse myself for my absence of concern. I long to appear visibly panicked, but it isn't my way. Not this man's way either. My friend coughs and some crumb-like substance flies out her mouth. My friend wipes her lips. She glances at the man with a look of gratitude then turns to me. I am looking at the man. He is already my beautiful creature.

"Thanks," I say.

"Anything to help."

"You were so fast."

"Well, you have to be, right?"

My friend touches my arm.

I try to wipe the smirk from my face. "You should eat with us," I say to the man. He looks embarrassed. He sits down anyway.

Over dinner, he regales us with adventures in doctoring—the pressures, the rewards. I only half listen. My full attention is on his large hands. They are strong, tan, and smooth like a glittering gem stone. Not an ounce of apprehension in them. All of this man is complete calm. I love it. My friend leaves. He leaves his friends. He walks me home.

On the sidewalk outside my apartment, he kisses me, the first kiss from a man, not a boy. It's different when it's a man. There still may be nerves, but they're nearly undetectable. A boldness is there instead, an acknowledgment of desire without doubt—a wet kiss. With a boy, it's dry.

We begin dating. There is an easiness to everything. It is so nice to be out with someone who can afford to pay for me. I can hold my own, but that's not the point. Without my powers and with Thomas paying for me, I finally convey the femininity I know I am capable of. We'd grab dinner on an overcast night in the city. Another day we take off for Santa Cruz and lie on the expansive beach. His assured nature and maturity make up for his lack of banter. I suspect he knows he does not need to say much. Lots of hand-holding; lots of kissing. Our first months together are over a dry July and August. An agitated sun glares down on Berkeley and Oakland, yet we seem happy. My new PR job is going well, but I mostly focus on the relationship.

In September, he changes. Something happens at the hospital in his second week after starting a new rotation. He won't tell me what occurred. I think he lost a patient. He opens the front door one day and avoids my gaze, instead heading straight for the fridge. He pulls out the loaf of bread along with the turkey meat and proceeds to make himself a sandwich, still without any recognition.

"What's wrong?" I ask. I expect a "nothing" or maybe

an "I'm fine." He says neither. "Thomas, look at me."

His eyes glaze over the chunky peanut butter he is spreading. He grasps the jar of jam like a lifeboat, my words an impending storm he can hear in the distance. I walk over to him, fighting the urge to run out of the room and never come back. "Tell me what happened," I say.

He finally looks up. "This guy, this patient."

"Yeah?"

I can see Thomas considering whether to tell me and then thinking better of it. He picks up a clean knife to cut his sandwich in two.

"Tell me."

In almost a whisper, Thomas says, "Just up and died."

"A patient died?"

Thomas nods.

"Was it your fault?" I know I shouldn't say that but can't help it.

He shakes his head.

"Hey." I try to hug him. He turns his shoulder away, toward the sandwich. He finishes cutting, then drops the knife and his shoulders. I manage to get my arms around him. "It will be okay," I say. "You want to go to bed?"

He looks at me, rather perplexed and a little troubled. "I have to go back to work."

"No, you don't."

"I think I should."

"Why?"

"I want to see what I did wrong."

"But you said you didn't do anything wrong."

His eyebrows furrow. "I must have done *something* wrong."

Thomas takes his sandwich to the living room and plops himself in front of the television. He's not going anywhere.

"I am going back," he says. "But I want to eat this sandwich first."

"Okay; I think that's a good idea."

"You do?"

I can't help but think how unimportant my own job is in comparison. I wish there is something I can do to help him, but we are not in the Parish.

He places his hand on mine. It is very warm. "I'll be okay once I eat this."

But he isn't. He doesn't return to the hospital that night. The next morning, he does not get out of bed. It is Friday, so I cannot afford to stay under the covers with him. He cannot afford to stay under either.

I return to our room wearing a towel, my wet hair dripping. I dry with another towel as I watch him, all childlike in the bed. He is curled up grasping the pillow like a stuffed animal. I consider dropping the towel I'm wearing but realize that wouldn't help any. "Are you going to get up?" I ask. My words are heavy and cumbersome as they escape my mouth.

"I don't think so."

"Why?"

"You go on ahead."

"I asked you why."

"Why do you think?"

"I really don't know. That's why I'm asking you."

He places the pillow over his head. He no longer seems older than me. I hate that. I try to hide the frustration from my voice. "Is there some investigation into what happened yesterday? At the hospital?"

"It's nothing like that."

"Then what is it?"

"What if it happens again?"

"What if *what* happens again?"

He looks at me like I can't understand simple arithmetic. "If I make a mistake?"

"Did you make a mistake before?"

He emerges from underneath the pillow. "I don't think so."

"Do they think you made a mistake?"

"No."

I sit on the bed, the damp towel still immersing my flesh. "Why would you make a mistake?"

"I don't know. But I can see myself making one. Can see it clearly. There's so many ways to make a mistake. And then what happens?"

"I'm not sure, Thomas," I say with an edge in my voice.

"Then it will be my fault."

I am losing the argument even though it is a stupid one. "Tell me this... Do the other doctors feel the same way? Like, wouldn't they hold the same concerns? The same fears?"

He shrugs his shoulders.

"Don't all of you encounter a certain degree of risk every day? Isn't risk part of the job?"

There is a long pause. Too long. He seems so far away, even though he is lying on the other side of the bed. I want to lean into the mattress, rest my head against my cushiony pillow. I fear if I lay down beside him, I won't get up and neither will he. His anxiety is an open wound I can't bear to look at. I ease off the bed. "You should go to work." I drop the towel and dress in front of him. He doesn't look at me.

I stop back at the apartment after lunch to see if he has left for the hospital. Thankfully he has. The next morning it is the same complaint, the same fears. His voice takes on a different resonance: an undercurrent of dread discharged through his ears. This time he lies face down on the bed.

"Thomas, if you just lie there and miss your shift they'll fire you."

"Is that all you care about?"

"What do you mean? I don't want you to get fired."

"I'm a doctor, you know."

His weakness—unattractive. His helplessness—some heavy appendage, a misshapen growth I cannot locate. I try a lighter tone nevertheless. "Doctors have to go to work, sweetheart."

He glares at some obscure crack in the ceiling which only he can see. "There's so much risk, you know. So much risk and we're all flying blind."

"You're not flying blind. You've been training for years."

"What good does it do if I can make a mistake?"

"Did you make a mistake?" I shouldn't say anything. It is so easy to get caught in his logic. Whatever ceiling crack he is focused on vanishes before him; he searches for a new crack among the crevices of white paint while the rage bubbles inside me.

"That's not the point," he says. "Every time I walk into the hospital and see a trusting look on some patient's face, I might be moments away from shedding that trust."

I am losing him—or rather he is losing himself. This time I pull up the sheets and slip inside the bed with him. Place my right hand on his burning forehead. "Breathe, Thomas. Can you do that for me?" I attempt to see things from his perspective, not because it is logical but in order to empathize. True empathy is new for me and so very hard to conjure. I try to glimpse the dread laid out in front of him, even though it is illogical, even though it could destroy him.

His arm stretches over me, pulls me closer to him underneath the covers. The warmness insulates us. We lie in silence, losing track of time, losing track of ourselves. Then I see it—for a brief moment, I can sense his fear, taste it with my tongue, a filmy vinegar—the watery poison—his poison. Even in San Francisco, I can still access a touch of my abilities. I discern in this moment what love is—my ability to experience this poison, allow it to transform me if need be, so I can feel what he does. Is this the kind of empathy people search for? The freeness to grieve with another person over their chilly, irrational, unforgiving failure? I start to choke back tears; my eye sockets water with his failure and my own shortcomings because I know I don't really want the joined companionship a real union could produce. I want my strength. I am not sure if I am grieving for the temporary loss of my strength and the wretched vulnerability which follows or grieving because I know I cannot offer what he seeks. I cannot practice the kind of love I know my beautiful creature requires.

So I depart the hilly streets of San Francisco and the promise of what people refer to as love. It takes weeks for my beautiful creature to leave his bedroom. I doubt there's anything I could have done to assist him. Better I return to the Parish where the thick air and scent of mildew has already commiserated together to plan my future.

Back in my apartment in the Parish, the hamburger meat on the stove is almost finished. I dump in the chopped onions—add a few dabs of ketchup. Sebastian will be here any minute. I'm reminded of the lesson my beautiful creature taught me whether he meant to or not. Guilt. He felt free to disperse it, to soften my defenses in the name of affection. He may have employed confidence at first. Those pale hazel eyes of his may have worked their magic on me. Still, the larger lesson is impossible to forget. My capacity to fear for him brought on greater guilt. Guilt can be employed for self-protection as well.

Phone chimes. He must be downstairs. I buzz him up. Check my hair in the mirror. Despite my best efforts, feel a vulnerability since Sebastian's visiting my apartment for the first time. Cannot be helped. The knock at the door. Close my eyes: maybe get a reading. Nothing. His heart rate is too rapid. Open the door for him. He looks like we've already spent the day together, like he's skipping the romance work. His tight lips reek of entitlement. He wants to kiss me. How childish. I lean in to let him hug me. Plop a kiss on his cheek. That will mess with him. Now he can wait while I finish dispersing my casserole into the serving bowl.

He paces. Wanders through the living room. Examines my book shelf, my Bronte novels—both sisters. He's judging some aspect of it all, though I'm unsure of what. Maybe he expects the books to be in some particular order. I'm the older one here. Does he think he's flirting? I want a guy who knows how to keep himself occupied without making me nervous. Sebastian looks out the window at a humming Decatur Street.

"Cool place."

"It's a great location."

"Definitely."

"All I have to do is walk outside, and I'm practically in the Quarter," I say.

"You go there often?" he asks.

I finish transferring the casserole into the bowl and smile. "Three or four times a week."

He nods as if he holds the same habits. He doesn't. "Would sure be something to live right in the Quarter," says the guy who still lives with his parents. He moves closer to the kitchen area. "Do you cook a lot?"

Not as much as I'd like. I arrive home pretty late from work.

"Like real late?"

"Late enough to not want to cook."

"I know what you mean," he says. I'm sure his mom cooks his meals. I'd ask, but confirmation could make him less attractive.

"Do you like being a substitute teacher?" I ask as I carry the casserole to the table, deliberately adding "substitute" to the title. I know he's not a real teacher.

"Yeah. I mean I like being a mentor."

"Is there opportunity for mentoring?"

"What do you mean?"

"I'm not sure," I say. "Depends on what you mean."

His eyebrows furrow like he's trying to read me. He won't be able to. Sebastian takes a breath as if he's about to give a formal talk. Hard to tell if he aims to deliver some inspirational wisdom or question my motives. He's kind of cute in the interim. I wish he wasn't a teacher, though. "I help the kids to see their potential. It's rewarding at times," he says. His comment feels genuine, surprising me. We sit down at the table. For a moment, Sebastian's a gazelle, his face relaxed and roving; doesn't appear as if he's about to say something, a relief for once.

We make small talk. He reveals more details about his job. The size of the theater class he subs for: twelve. The number of fellow faculty members who speak to him: two. How he feels to be teaching at his own high school: weird. Once he begins to talk, he doesn't stop. Difficult to discern whether this is a nervous tic of his or if he really appreciates the sound of his own voice. I wish he'd ask me more about myself. Hate him a little for making me feel that way. It's not like I'm sitting here, chewing on my mediocre casserole, desperately needing to share my life, but rather, his unwillingness to inquire about my own trials makes me feel disregarded as a person, as if he is the movie star and I am the makeup girl. The way his lips fold in on themselves suggest an unbridled smugness—he's the kid in the summer camp cabin everyone probably hated. And pummeled in the evening.

Knowing he lacks the ability adds to my frustration. If I were smart, I'd be relieved at his shortcoming. If he held the ability, how could a relationship really exist with such a dangerous dynamic? Would I want to contend with such a burden? I wonder how many more dates we'll go on. Regardless of any Society connection, I need to be with a man.

He surprisingly takes my plate along with his own to

the kitchen; scrubs them off in the sink before placing them in the dishwasher. His dash of masculinity initiates a slight quiver. We move to the couch. His knee brushes against mine. As I turn on the television, he grins like a nurse measuring my height. "I have a job opportunity," he says.

He must know I don't care for his teaching, but drawing further attention to the fact will not impress me. "What kind of opportunity?" I ask.

"Do you like golf?"

"I've played a few times."

"My brother and I used to play. Strike that. I played. Practiced a lot, actually. My brother and father dabbled. My brother has a terrible swing."

"Doesn't your brother live in Los Angeles?"

He nods, hoping to avoid further inquiry.

"Does he like it?" I ask.

"I don't really talk to him."

"Why's that?"

"He's pretty into himself."

"Aren't most guys?"

He smiles. "That's funny."

"I'm serious."

He notices his knee is touching mine. He shifts his body toward me. "My brother acts like my dad. It finally got to be too much, you know. Because he needs my parents just as much as I do, even though he pretends otherwise." He breathes out in an attempt to project calm in spite of his mini outburst. Sebastian rests his hand on my arm. I feel the bygone rush of San Francisco unfold around me for a moment. "Have you heard of Skip Mackadoo?" he asks.

"Should I?"

"Depends if you like golf?"

"I've only played mini-golf."

Sebastian's voice expands in certainty. "He's a major golfer on the pro tour. Mackadoo is a personality. Infectious smile. Total adrenaline. Loves to work the crowd."

"Like Happy Gilmore?"

"Kind of. He *could* be like that. With the right guidance."

"Is he good?"

"At golf?"

I nod vigorously, attempting to shield my sarcasm. "Yeah, you said he's a pro golfer."

"The guy possesses a graceful swing. When he's on a roll, he summons a fire in his gut. The problem is he's too inconsistent to capture the large following he's capable of generating."

"So he has to practice more."

"I think it's more about confidence. And performance."

"What do you mean, 'performance?' Golf performance?"

"He holds the talent to maintain interest. I can help him hone this talent."

"I don't understand. You're not a golf teacher?"

"I'm an acting teacher."

I like seeing him excited about something, but his lack of clarity makes my blood thicken. "Where are you going with this, Sebastian?"

He beams like he just opened the Christmas present he was hoping for. "I met Mackadoo on the driving range the other day. Made him a pitch on how he can better generate interest."

It's almost impossible not to smile at Sebastian's assuredness, so I do. "What did he say?"

"He offered me a job."

"Really?"

"Going to be his performance coach."

"For golf?"

"Exactly."

"What about your teaching job at Alabaster? You're in the middle of the school year."

His eyes register a hint of anger, but then he smiles. "This is in addition to that."

"So it's part-time?"

Sebastian nods. "The position will be a trial run. I'll work with him every time he has a tournament in the south. We'll see how it goes. If he likes what I do, then he said he'll hire me full time. Most of gigs will be on the weekends, so it shouldn't interfere with school too much."

"It sounds perfect."

"I know, right?" He uses the opportunity to take my hand. He kisses it. I don't mind. He really is charming when he makes an effort.

"Did you tell your brother?"

"Why do you ask that?" he says, trying not to appear annoyed, even though he obviously is.

"No reason," I say innocently.

"I don't talk to him."

"Okay. What about your parents?"

He looks at me a moment like he's reaching for something. "I wanted to tell you first."

I kiss him on the lips. "Well, thank you for telling me.

I'm really excited for you."

"Thank you," he says, genuinely pleased.

MOIRA

2022

BLUE AND WHITE regal awnings and majestic white columns shelter us from the cold glare of the public. The Society holds a long relationship with the restaurant. Renting the place out for meetings, negotiations, and celebrations affords us secrecy and neutral ground. A festive mood permeates the sprawling maroon-walled dining room. Sebastian smiles like a newly minted citizen, his sense of belonging deep. Victor's in fine spirits too, particularly in watching my baby boy's soft little head nearly float above his body, leaning into his significant other like she's some warm life jacket. To see a confidence newly born into one's son must be gratifying for Victor. My dress shoes press into the teal carpeting; heels twist in silent protest of Addison Liondale, who sits across from me in a tart magenta dress, revealing too much for my tastes though I'm sure Sebastian is thrilled, and Victor's isn't too broken up about it either. One's life jacket may be another's irritant. Addison regales us with tales of her time in San Francisco, her Generation Z struggles to alleviate some degree of poverty in the Castro District during her volunteer endeavors. I know in my heart without even reading her that she intends to become Raymond's successor. I read her anyway. Reach out over the saccharine turtle soup, bend around the half-filled wine glasses, my invisible hand a bludgeon if I can breach her consciousness. Can feel her blocking me. Is that a wink in my direction? Recoil in an instant; she commands more control than I imagined. Why couldn't I pick up on this before? Regret our decision to match her with Sebastian, who's far too self-absorbed to detect her subterfuge. Why did we agree to this? To instill some sense of direction in our son? Can this girl really fix his arrested development? At what cost? She gestures with her hands, concocting sweeping motions when she speaks. Carries a vague something not of the Parish about her. It's not the time in the Bay area either. It resides in her speech—the way she manages to turn discussions back to herself. She's what you'd call charming if I were to ever call a person that word. But charming only works when describing a stranger, their ability to make you like them in those fleeting moments in order to get what they want. Charming cannot operate over longer periods of time. It becomes tiresome. A lanky waiter arrives to collect our main course plates. He glances at me and nods. He ignores Victor. I appreciate the gesture. How far I've come. I must remind myself that as Ms. Liondale continues to espouse on the virtues of community involvement, even though I know she's never lifted a finger in our own city to aid the less fortunate, I'm reminded of my own sense of displacement when I was introduced to The Society. Remember the sheer unreality of it all, how the system joined together on several fronts in order to preserve the essence of what makes the city special. Ms. Liondale never had to endure this displacement because of who her uncle is. I wonder if she realizes her uncle is the one who introduced it all to me? Look at Sebastian watching her prattle. What did I do wrong? Know the answer to the question, of course. Once Ms. Liondale begins discussing her admiration for her uncle, it's time to mix this dinner up. "Sebastian, tell us more about this new job opportunity," I say. "We're here tonight to celebrate you, after all."

Ms. Liondale turns to Sebastian. She smirks, showing too much of her teeth for the motion to be genuine.

"I start in a week," he says, pride springing from his voice.

"Won't you need to miss some school?" Victor asks.

"Only a handful of times when I need to be at a match on Fridays."

Victor tries not to sound concerned. "Sounds like more than a few."

"I've got it covered."

"I think it's great Sebastian's branching out from teaching," Ms. Liondale says.

I smile too broadly. "Why do you say that?"

"Well, aren't you excited about the potential for growth?" she says to me.

"You don't think a teacher grows? In what they do every day?"

"I didn't mean it like that?"

"I see."

"You meant responsibility," Victor says, trying to help.

"Right."

"So helping one golfer," I say, "not at the top of his

game, compensate by putting on a show suggests greater responsibility than being in charge of fifteen students?"

She stiffens. "Mrs. Levinson, I'm supportive of Sebastian's new opportunity. And I'm excited for him."

Victor grins at Sebastian. "We all are."

I look at my clueless son. If I were capable of shedding a tear for him right at the table, at our special restaurant where paintings of smug ancestors in The Society look judgingly down on us, I would. Instead, I give Ms. Liondale's wine glass the slightest push a half-second before she picks it up, causing the glass to spill towards her.

"Oh, gosh," she calls out, the sticky bubbles slipping onto her wrist.

Sebastian grabs his napkin and Victor's. "Let me help you." The river of red flows toward Liondale; a drop falls in her lap. She takes a napkin from Sebastian and dabs her dress. Her eyes meet mine. She knows, but there's no way to prove it.

I smile helpfully, like I'm cheering for her to win a 100 meter. "Sebastian, you're such a gentleman. You're going to do such a great job helping that golfer."

The waiter arrives and attends to the table with dabs of wet napkin. He catches my attention with his wandering eye. When he finishes with the mess, he brings his hand to his chin. "A moment, madame."

I throw Victor a look of reassurance I will return, purposely avoiding eye contact with Sebastian or Liondale. I follow the waiter into the next-door dining room.

"You have a message," the waiter says. "I will get him."

"We blocked out the restaurant. This is a private dinner. Where did this *messenger* come from?"

Raymond appears from behind a corner. "The service entrance," he bellows. He sips a cappuccino. "What course are you on?" he asks with interest.

"What are you doing here?"

"Celebrating your son."

"Stop."

He brightens. "You getting to know my niece?"

"The best I can."

"What is *that* supposed to mean?"

I shake my head in dismissal.

Raymond nods, satisfied with the stalemate. He takes another sip of his cappuccino. "You know, the first time the restaurant was used as a meeting place, we negotiated with the Spanish for control of the city. We invited them here to discuss terms. Supposedly, everyone had turtle soup and venison."

I wink at him. "I like how you use the word, *we*."

"Well, it's true. They're our ancestors."

"You're from New Haven."

"It hurts me when you say that. You know very well they're my ancestors. And yours." He leans against one of the maroon walls. I'm wearing tight black slacks, and I see him looking. It's not lost on me the restaurant used to be a brothel in the 1700s. His eyes wander with a luxuriousness and recklessness only afforded the highly privileged.

"What's the story on your niece?"

"What about her?" he says defensively.

"Something's rotten in the state of Denmark."

He nods, smiling. "She's not my daughter. She's my

niece. I did not raise her."

"So you're blaming your sister for the girl's upbringing?"

"Absolutely not. Is she getting on your nerves?"

"You could say that."

"What a shame. Your son should be so lucky to spend his days with someone of her ability."

"Leave Sebastian out of it."

"Why? It's unusual to hold zero ability with parents like his."

"Are you complimenting Victor?"

He shakes his head. "Only stating a fact."

"I'd like to get back to my dinner."

"What a lie." He wears regret on his face like a child who's behaved abominably in front of his mother but still doesn't care. Raymond sits down on the edge of the mahogany fireplace, which likely hasn't been activated in 100 years. "Why did you withdraw?" he asks in a quiet voice. "From everything? We were making such progress."

"It's funny you use that word."

"What?"

"Progress. I thought our role was to protect the city from itself. Can you honestly say you've achieved that?"

"I have accomplished many great things—"

"Name some." His ensuing silence makes the room feel like it's about to decompose. Our disagreement runs straight to the root. He's been an ineffective steward of the Parish, though lately, he's been a cog in the city's circulation.

"I think we've made steady progress to fortify the Parish after the latest hurricane."

"You prevented Victor from building the new levee.

His design would save lives. And why? Jealousy?"

"Everything attached to construction is more complicated than you describe."

"You make it sound harder than it is."

"Is this your way of asking to return to the fold?"

My head shakes in disappointment. Hard to forget how enamored I was in his presence. We'd walk the streets of the Quarter at dusk, and I'd think—*where did this person come from?*

"You used to be so captivated by it all," he says.

"Don't read my mind." I move closer to him. "I was only twenty-one. What did you expect?" For a moment, the silence of the ancient room engulfs us. I imagine early members here, striking deals with robber barons. Can smell their rough tobacco, the inside leather of their boots, still damp with sweat from riding. "Why are you here? I'd like to get back to dinner."

He runs his fingers through hair as white as powdered donuts. "Carson."

"What about him?"

"How's he doing?"

"He's fine."

"Not what I hear."

I make a face. "You've recently been to Los Angeles?"

"Don't ask questions you know I won't answer." He rests his cappuccino cup on the edge of the fireplace and rises. "I hear he wants to return."

Remembering Sebastian with Ms. Liondale in the other room makes the prospect sound appealing.

"He already made the choice," Raymond points at me. "You already made it for him."

"I've made no such choice." I look him over. "You're

afraid of him?"

"Staying in LA will be better...for everyone."

"I miss my son."

"So visit him. I have excellent restaurant re-commendations for Malibu." He turns his back to me to leave but ceases to take a step. "I want my niece to succeed me when it's time. If Sebastian lasts, it will be good for your family." The velvet carpet crinkles under his feet, and despite his best efforts, he betrays a slight shuffle in his step. There's still subtle menace in the way he leads with his shoulders, but he's not what he once was. His withdrawal from the room leaves a bleakness in its wake. I want peace for my sons—a potential Carson return would be anything but.

I re-enter the dining room, but instead of walking to the table, I watch them all. They're smiling, chatting with a breezy intimacy, the tension and pressure dried by a warm sun after the storm—my exit from the table. Yet, on closer inspection, I find Liondale doing much of the talking; her generous gestures make sharp angles, all directed at Victor. Sebastian leans back in his chair, likely oblivious to his date's overt flirtations with his father. I've positioned my baby boy in this situation, not simply with the new girlfriend, but with this new life of his. He also needed to leave, but unlike Carson, I've kept him here because of my own selfish actions. Couldn't bear to see both of them leave.

I return to a table in mid-conversation propelled by Ms. Addison Liondale. As Sebastian looks on in lonely wonderment, I realize my lack of focus on my son has enacted further damage. Sebastian's hitched himself to a creature with a self-interest that surpasses his own. If I knew how to talk to him, I'd have the match dissolved. When he looks at her with childish awe, I see someone who may not love him but who will go through the requisite motions. She'll make it seem like love. I gather it may be too late.

MOIRA

2021

SEBASTIAN'S EXAMS ARE all finished at the end of his junior year, one year prior to Carson's move to Los Angeles. The May humidity in the Parish attaches to my thighs and ankles. Wet heat in spring is always a sign of tumultuous change; hard to discern where it will come from. Overjoyed students emerge from their last classes while others load Rubbermaid containers into their cars. The end is in sight. Empty vertically piled boxes lie in wait outside the front door of Sebastian's apartment-style dormitory. His resident advisor nervously provides directions to parents, likely hoping there will be no confrontations for his gross negligence during the school year. Victor volunteers to load incidentals into the SUV, conveniently missing Sebastian's tour. I suspect he wants to remove himself from any potential conflict between the twins. A satisfied Sebastian leads Carson and me along the pedestrian walkway. This is Carson's first time on campus since Sebastian was a freshman, and Sebastian is anxious to show him the important sights where he's spent the last three years. Sebastian couldn't wait to visit Carson a handful of times in New York, but Carson never stops by the campus in later seasons even when he's home for the holidays. He always maintains some excuse. Eventually, Sebastian stops asking. Sebastian enjoys sharing Carson with others as he grows older; he introduces Carson as his more centered, more confident fraternal twin. A slight manic quality resides under Sebastian's words as he guides us past the University Center, its sizeable windows gathering Louisiana sunlight in its warm embrace. What should be a fun time of reunion is fraught with uncertainty. No one should stare down graduation in a year without a plan in place for the crucial next steps. I am to blame for Sebastian's lack of preparation: all my worry concentrated on Carson instead and his need to remain away from the Parish before his abilities come to fruition. He already placed so much dedication into his screenwriting, and I know he has his heart set on Los Angeles. Then of course is the other issue. It isn't just that his powers will fully materialize. He will eventually be expected to lead. Or more likely, others will demand he defend his right to lead, Raymond's niece the most likely immediate threat besides Raymond himself. I can feel her drive, a sophistication and hunger unencumbered by restraint. I've never seen the same longing from Carson. He would need to really want The Society if he were to stay. Then again, we've shielded much from the boys for their own protection. We've allowed Carson to pursue his dream. Why stop now?

Sebastian, on the other hand, holds minimal ideas for the future, and I've yet to help him brainstorm. To overcompensate for a vague future lying before him, he throws himself into this impromptu campus tour, a tour requiring an enthusiastic buy-in Carson is ill-equipped to provide his brother.

We cross Ferret Street, an outdoor oasis of greenery and no-man's-land siphoned off from the hustle and bustle of campus. Sebastian wants to show us Gibson Hall at the front of the school where the streetcar crosses. Sebastian forgets I went here too, but in three years, I do little to remind him of the fact—another wasted opportunity to bond with my son.

Carson points to a cream-colored, colonial-looking structure. "Isn't that the English building?" he asks his brother.

"No, it's the Gothic-looking one next door. You want to see it?" Sebastian asks.

Carson already begins walking toward the building; he passes eager students in polos and shorts on the way to begin their packing. Carson walks with a confident stride, wearing navy blue topsiders without socks. He thinks they make him appear grown-up, which they inevitably do. We stop at the archway. Carson rests on the bench and stretches his arms as if he were a current student. "Didn't I take a class here one summer? In high school?"

"You did. An American Literature course," I say.

Sebastian twitches. Somehow, with one comment, Carson manages to make the tour about himself. Sebastian attempts to regain his tour guide momentum. "I've taken a few classes here too."

"Only a few?" Carson says. "It's a strong department."

"If it's so strong, why didn't you go here?"

"What's that supposed to mean?"

"I would think twins would want to go to college together."

"We're graduating in less than a year. Why bring this up now?"

"'Cause it still hurts."

"Sebastian, it was important for me to go to New York for the writing program."

"Sure it was."

A student eyes them suspiciously as he passes.

"Come on, guys," I say with annoyance.

Carson shakes his head. "I took care of you enough in high school."

Sebastian waves him off and begins to pace. "Wait a minute, wait a minute."

"Don't act so puzzled. You know what I'm talking about."

"Uh, I really don't."

"I'm not surprised considering your low self-awareness," Carson says.

I stare out at the quad. Students deftly make an effort to avoid walking toward us as they double down on their conversations in progress. "Sebastian, let's see the theater building," I say.

"Yeah, Sebastian; show us the center of make-believe."

"Carson, that was ugly," I say. "Your long-term focus is writing. How can you call the theater building make-believe?"

My youngest by a hair tries to grin like a card player holding a lousy hand. "What do you mean, 'long term focus'?"

"You know what I mean," I say warily. "It's what his degree will be in."

Carson snorts. "It's more than that, Sebastian."

"Tell me," Sebastian says.

"There's a good chance I'm heading to LA next year."

I cringe at Carson's words, knowing they will set Sebastian off for sure.

Sebastian nods like the news is the most logical revelation in the world. "Who's going to pay for that?" he asks. As if that's any of his business.

Carson gazes down across the walkway, no doubt waiting for me to answer.

Sebastian smiles, breathing in his compact campus in his compact world—his place of refuge, which can no longer shield him from undetermined life advancing before him.

"We will pay for it, if he ends up going," I finally say in a quiet voice. "It's not decided yet."

"It's practically decided," Carson says.

Thinking of Raymond and his niece when I hear him say that, I can't help but be relieved.

Sebastian looks at us like he's visiting another family. "What about me?"

"What *about* you?" Carson says.

"That's enough," I say. "We're not having this conversation here."

"Hey, I'd sure like to have it somewhere," Sebastian says.

I gesture for them to follow me. I lead my sons around Gibson to the greeny front of campus. We sit on the dry grass, facing the streetcar tracks, the oak trees affording us a drop of privacy. "It's important Carson leaves the city at this critical time," I say. I look at Sebastian, hoping to catch a snippet of empathy before it flutters away. "So Carson isn't recruited by The Society."

"What does this have to do with me?"

Carson glares at him. "It doesn't. Why does everything have to do with you?"

"Can I go to LA too?"

Carson smiles. "To act, Sebastian?"

Here are my two sons, my baby boys, my twinly twosome, on the way to tearing each other apart. Their animosity grows by the minute. And why? Because talent and intelligence were dispersed unequally, the cruel inequity of birth finally receiving the public airing it always longed for.

Sebastian stands up in the grass. "You bet, to act. You know I want to be a college acting teacher, but I need more experience before I go to grad school."

Carson maintains a measured tone. "So you think LA would be a good place for you to act in some plays?"

"Definitely."

"They don't have plays there." Carson catches my gaze; he wipes his watery eyelids. He seems to be weighing the pitfalls of pressing on in his attack. He wants to go to Los Angeles alone. From Carson's perspective, it is more important for Sebastian to see he is wrong about himself than for Carson to be right. "What roles did you play in college?" Carson asks.

"I was in *Enemy of the People*."

"You play Hovstad?"

A look of disappointment flashes across Sebastian's face. "You know who I played."

The mother in me wants to stop Carson. Five minutes earlier, Sebastian embodied the triumphant college veteran, taking his family on one last tour through his well-worn stomping grounds. Now I allow Carson to ruin any positive memory Sebastian will have of this day. On the other hand, I long to see how Carson will handle himself—can he do what is necessary to reach his brother, which could help Sebastian in the end? Does Carson hold the stamina to ambush when necessary? He'll need the skill one way or the other.

Sebastian looks directly at his brother. "I was The Drunk in that play."

Carson grins. "That's right. You swayed around a lot on the DVD."

I turn to Sebastian, pleased when I see his face harden, ready to fight back against his brother. As he ages in the Parish, he'll need to defend himself against everyone with abilities.

"I stole the show," Sebastian says to his skeptical brother. "You'd know that if you had seen the production in person."

"What role did you have afterwards?" Carson asks.

"I was in *Death of a Salesman*," Sebastian finally says. "I played Bernard."

Carson repeats the character's name like it's some peculiar hotel.

"It's a pivotal role," Sebastian protests.

"It's an important role; I wouldn't say it's a pivotal role. It's not Biff's brother, Happy. Or Biff. Why weren't you one of the major roles?"

Sebastian shakes his head. "What do you want me to say, Carson? I didn't get the part." Sebastian looks to me for help. I smile at him; he lowers his head in disappointment at me.

"If you struggle to snag a lead role here, why would it be easier in Los Angeles, auditioning for film?" Carson asks.

"No one said it would be easier."

"Do you realize the level of competition you'll be up against?"

"This is about you not wanting me with you in LA."

Carson rises to face him. "No, this is about you only mentioning LA the moment you discovered *I* was going to LA."

"It's not my fault, you, Mom, and Dad are keeping it a secret."

"No one's keeping it a secret," I say frivolously.

"This is about you not having a plan, brother," Carson says, pointing his finger at him. "Not until exactly one minute ago when you discovered my plan and turned it into your own."

Sebastian pushes him. "Stop it."

Two reasons come to mind as to why I don't halt my boys from doing irreparable damage to their relationship, let alone continue to allow Carson to dismantle Sebastian's considerable self-confidence—I want my Carson to focus on his writing; he mustn't worry over Sebastian's schemes and the likely pitfalls to follow. Another point to consider: if Sebastian stays in the Parish, I can make up for lost time, help him find a suitable profession, try to repair the cavernous gulf between us. The gulf sneaks up on me one morning at the crack of dawn—my irises feel dry and raw from lack of sleep during the chaos and responsibilities of winter break. On our porch, I stare at the inadequate levee and wonder, *how do you show love to two children equally when you need to attend to one far more than the other?* The gulf may have been a crevice at first, but now it is a bog with swamp water beginning to ferment. My monitoring of Carson's developing abilities and my efforts to keep Raymond at bay come at a cost. During dinner the night before the college tour, when Sebastian begins to tell us about his latest college acting project, I can sense the elaboration in his voice, the restless yearning for validation, which can only be achieved through unadulterated verbal domination. His vocal pitch pushes down any foreign sounds. He looks over at me in between bites of his red beans and rice. What should be a son's desire for a mother's approval is instead a silent acknowledgment he doesn't really need it—that he only requires me to listen and produce the necessary gestures he desires.

Yet, one look at Sebastian's proud stance in the hot grass in front of Gibson Hall, in spite of the embarrassing observations Carson has made, reveals to me the extent to which I no longer know my son like I thought I would. Remorse and rage flush scarlet across Sebastian's cheeks: remorse over his inability to articulate his own hopes and dreams—rage over the impracticality of it all. Meanwhile, Carson's failure to resist criticizing his brother results in its own consequences. He neglects to see Sebastian slowly advancing toward him as Sebastian begins to whisper under his breath. Naturally, Carson wants to hear what his brother is telling him, so he edges closer, which is when Sebastian lunges for his stomach, tackling Carson to the ground. Carson flails as Sebastian punches him in the gut.

"Stop it," I yell. I look behind me. Luckily no one is out front, but cars continue to pass on Saint Charles. I can hear the incoming vibration and steady chime of the streetcar in the distance. "That's enough. Both of you," I say. By this point, Carson tries to get on top of Sebastian, albeit unsuccessfully. I can't risk Sebastian's university standing falling into jeopardy; close my eyes. Both my sons, just as they reach a standing position, have the gravity pulled out from under them. They each take a tumble. Sebastian doesn't know what has happened, but Carson looks up at me in wonder. I'll need to separate them on a larger scale.

CARSON

2022

THE BEACH IS a good place to say goodbye. Upon arrival in LA, I imagined I would grow old here, alone: ocean breeze procured in abundance. Wrinkled toes sneaking through sand, I'd rub my expanded belly in quiet satisfaction, proud at what I'd accomplished. Would stand among the young people playing volleyball, smiling for the willpower to skip those moments of carefree opportunity during my own youth, opting instead for solitary bouts of ingenuity. I would look back, satiated from productive years on my screenwriting journey, occasionally achieving creations of fantastical entertainment. None of that will reach fruition now. I make a last-ditch effort for some kind of mark on the place I grew up idolizing and dreaming about, a place that quietly unravels me from the inside.

Entering Pacific Palisades in my Jetta brings a sense of perspective. The cliffs sink below the car like readied quicksand. I turn the wheel and navigate along what feels like a mountain because it's close to one, creating the sensation of falling. The wheels grip the road, pulling the car upward through unadulterated acceleration. This spot comes off as mystical, separated from the rest of Los

Angeles by a never-ending Sunset Boulevard: the non-famous part of it. This neighborhood is the ideal place to start a cult. Trees hide the daily goings-on, but wealth lingers everywhere like hot coffee on the tongue.

The canyon the oligarch's property sits on appears colossal in the sobering light of day. On the night of the party, you could hear the rhythms of anticipation wind their way out the bay windows. No jubilant beats syncopate now, only the blaring alarm system, which screeches through palm trees as I rush through the yard. I expect nothing for the first time ever, so it's surprising when a six-foot-four bodybuilder decks me right before my hand reaches the knob of the front door. "Where did you come from?" I cry from the ground, my lip puffed with blood.

"Get up," he says, not at all interested in conversation.

"I want to see the oligarch."

"That's not his name."

"So I can see Demetri?"

He kicks me in the side. "Not when you trespass."

"I was going to ring the doorbell."

"Shut up."

I wipe the blood from my lip and look up at him. He sees I lack any power in the situation; his expression changes to one of curiosity.

"I'll tell him you're outside."

The library is substantial, but there's something off about it, like maybe Demetri has only gently perused the majority of the books on the shelf. There's a blood leather chair facing the window, a snippet of the ocean visible in the distance. The last glint of day dissolves before

Demetri finally enters.

"Welcome to my home," he gestures with his wide forearms.

"Thanks for having me."

"Well, you trespassed."

"I stopped by," I say.

"When you're rich, it's trespassing."

I nod, wondering if I already made a major mistake. "I wanted to talk to you."

"Ballsy."

"Probably."

"Paolan said you did a—what were his words? *Mediocre* job on the script."

"I suppose he said he'll have to re-write the thing himself."

"He did say that. So, I said, at least you don't have to write the thing from scratch. Are you here to tell me it was not a mediocre job?"

"It was an excellent job," I say.

Demetri bows his head. "Your modesty speaks volumes."

"Is modesty really the best quality when I'm trying to sell myself?"

He gestures for me to sit in the leather chair. He grabs a roll-out computer chair for himself that looks cushiony and expensive with loads of adjustments. "Are we trying to sell ourselves or tell the truth?"

"I'm doing both."

"That's the conundrum with this place. Few get to do both."

"If you'd like me to make revisions, I can do that."

"I'm not a producer. That's why I hired Paolan."

He's got me there. Now I feel like I'm going around my boss, which I am, but Paolan's not really my boss as he wants nothing to do with me. He's got the script in his hands now. Plus the legal thing.

"I received a letter from Paolan's lawyer," I say.

Demetri's eyes widen; he seems genuinely surprised.

"It basically says the script was his idea, his story, and he only hired me to write the script. It also says—"

"Were you paid?"

"What?"

Demetri leans in. "I said, were you paid?"

"No."

He shakes his head. "I'm impressed."

I realize what he means, but I still clarify. "With Paolan?"

"Of course. He's complaining about the job you did, but he neglected to pay you." Demetri leans back in his chair as if the conflict is solved. "That is why you are angry."

"I'm not angry," I say. "I wanted to make a movie."

"Is it his idea?"

"The idea? Sure. The kernel of the idea, if you make a pitch in a room—in the first ten seconds. But I created the characters, their personalities, the story structure—mostly everything. I copyrighted it."

"He let you copyright it?"

"Told me to take whatever precautions I believed were necessary."

Demetri laughs. "What a fool."

"I took precautions."

"No, him." He points at me with mild amusement. "And I suppose you informed him of the precautions you took."

"The other night."

"You cannot fault him for trying to steal the script from you."

"Why not?"

"It's how this town works."

His honesty's disturbing and reassuring at the same time. I imagine his willingness to level with me somehow translates to solving a problem. It doesn't. "So I'm here to give you the script to read yourself."

"The one Paolan doesn't like?"

"He doesn't like it because he couldn't put his stamp on it. Yet."

Demetri smiles at me. "You prepared for this. Good for you."

"So you'll read it?"

"No."

"I assure you; it's excellent."

"I'm not going to read it because it will never be made." He rises from his expensive computer chair and shakes his head. "It's too high a budget."

"It can be lowered."

"I do not make movies."

Feel the conversation slipping into dangerous terrain, but at the same time, I'm comfortable talking with him. This in itself is perilous because I shouldn't be talking with him at all.

"You mean, you don't make the business decisions?"

"Kid, we don't make movies. That film you saw a few months back—it'll never see a theater."

"But you made the movie."

"Sure we made it. Money's got to go somewhere." He winks, and there it is. It was finally clear they were using the films to launder money. Lots of it. My script was just another cover. That still didn't explain Paolan's trickery.

"Why would Paolan steal the script from me if you're not going to make it anyway? Doesn't he know?"

"Sure he knows. Yes, we made the film you saw. Occasionally we need to make one. Otherwise it all starts to look suspicious. Maybe he doesn't want you taking the script somewhere else."

"How would I sell it if he makes me believe I've failed?"

He grins at me. We nod in silent agreement. This rumpled mobster with the luxurious computer chair has leveled with me, the first to do so in LA. I feel indebted to him. He can sense it.

"Of course, I can't have screenwriters walking around town knowing how I conduct my business."

"What do you mean?"

"Carson, what do you think I mean?" It's the first time he's used my name. It's jarring to my ears like some obnoxious neighbor pounding on the floor above me. Except the neighbor carries a gun. "You know facts. Facts which cannot leave this property." He pauses, lifts his chin so I can see the gray stubble underneath his lip. "Would you like to leave the property?" The way he punctuates his consonant sounds pounds violence against the room's air circulation.

I consider what it would look like to start running. Wouldn't be pretty. Not even sure where the front door is.

"How will you fix this problem?" he asks. Lovely. I'm setting him up for understandable hostility on his end. Ignorance might be my best bet. It works for everyone else.

"I'm not even sure what you told me," I say.

"You're not being genuine," he says with an air of disappointment.

"What did you tell me exactly?" For some reason I believe not remembering will amend the situation.

"That will not work." His cheeks inflate, his teeth whiter than I expect. "Make me an offer, Carson, and I'll make you one in return. That's what we do in this town. We do not wait. Paolan does. He won't last."

"I'd like you to buy my screenplay. My version. The better one."

"How much?"

"Two hundred."

"Two hundred thousand?"

I recoil upon hearing the number aloud, even though his additional digit is part of my initial offer. I nod.

He moves toward his bar; it's a complete set-up I didn't see when I entered the room. He produces two glasses and grabs a bottle with a fancy label—it's got a silhouette of a confident-looking horse. "I will purchase the script for $150,000."

I focus on the shine from the glass, trying not to look pleased. Grateful I'm not being taken advantage of, particularly because negotiation is off the table.

"Congratulations on your first sale." He toasts me. "And likely your last for a while. Your exodus from Los Angeles in thirty-six hours..." he looks at his watch, a glistening Patek Phillipe, "begins now."

"Thirty-six hours?"

"Is generous. I can't have you waltzing around town knowing how I run my operation. Unfortunately, you figured it out."

"You told me!"

He shakes his head, a deft signal to lower my voice. I oblige. "You're wasting your life here anyway."

"How do you figure?"

"It's not about the work. Should be clear to you by now."

"I was the strongest writer in my screenwriting class."

Demetri bursts out laughing. His laugh turns into a surprising giggle; he grabs the base of the bar for support. I've hit a nerve. I should be more cautious, make an effort to find my way to the door, yet his ridicule stings. He gestures at me. "The boy says he's talented. Stop the presses."

"I have just as much right as anyone in this town to establish myself," I say.

He laughs again. "Paolan said your script is about a secret society in Boston. I have never been to Boston." He downs his glass. "I have been to Orleans Parish, though."

I look at floor. "I don't follow."

"The secret society you write about? It's in Orleans Parish, yes?"

"No, Boston," I say defensively.

"In the script, yes. Not in real life." He swallows some of the liquor from what was supposed to be my glass. "Paolan doesn't have a clue who you are. I do."

"You mean my father?"

"Paolan's South African nobility pales in comparison to yours."

"Okay."

"It's the reason I will let you flee." He looks at his watch once again. "You better be going."

In a city of opportunity, thirty-six hours is still a lift to shut down a life, even if it's a shell of an adult's life. With no further calls from Paolan or Demetri, I'm left with enough time to secure a moving company as well as a cross-country trucking service, which agreed to transport my car to the Parish. I'm well aware Mom didn't want me spending my young adulthood there. I can always bill my stay as a temporary stop on the way to the next thing. The semi-truck sits at the curb on Montana and 7th Street, looking like an odd sky-blue rectangular portal to another life I tried to avoid until now. I pull the Jetta over to the side of the road behind the truck and stare at the back of the trailer. Feel like loading myself along with the car onto the inviting ramp, an industrial size cocoon I can hide my failure in. Even with the money, it's still a failure. I step out of the car and focus on the shiny glint of my California license plate as it disappears onto the electric ramp inside the truck. Twenty-four hours left. Without a car, I really am grounded. Half of me's already back in the Parish, ready to face whatever The Society has in store. Pass the Brentwood Mart on foot. Young families and professionals scoop their mint chip and pistachio in the glare of the Santa Monica sun peeking out among the haze. What do these young professionals possess that I do not? A steady job? Then again, it's three in the afternoon. What are they doing at this hour savoring soft, sweet ice cream on the veranda? Perhaps they're pretending as well. Maybe everyone here pretends. Of course they do—should know that by now.

As I maneuver the curved streets of Barrington where

the palm trees hang like a broken volleyball net, I think of Sebastian and wonder how he's doing. Look forward to seeing him and hearing his BS. My eyelash twitches, for a second, I feel he's in danger. It passes.

A block from my apartment, I notice a shadow of a figure through the palm trees, pacing outside my place. Looks like Tighe, my manager. Hard to be sure in the light. Upon closer inspection, it is Tighe, a stocky man in his late twenties who looks like he used to play football in high school but switched out the football for pitchers of Budweiser. He still attempts to carry himself like a winning jock even though the slump in his step gives him away. He forecasts a laziness that says he cannot really be bothered to emerge from his bed. He'd like to be a power agent with thirty years of industry experience. He's not. He's only a few years older than me.

He brightens when he sees me. "It's the guy."

I eye him suspiciously. He stopped returning my calls once Paolan decided he didn't like my script. "How long have you been waiting for me?"

"Not long, man, not long. Whatcha up to?"

I wipe a drop of sweat from my forehead; I can feel the sunburn forming at the back of my neck. "Taking a walk." I've been on foot way longer than some casual stroll. Do not feel like revealing what I just did with my Jetta.

Tighe nods like he knows where I was anyways. "What happened with Paolan's script?"

"*Paolan's* script?" I say incredulously.

"The script you wrote," he repeats with a laudatory effect.

"Shouldn't you know the answer to that since you're my manager?"

"You want to go inside?" he asks with a coaxing air.

"I'd rather not. What's up?"

He bites his lip. "I know you worked hard on that script."

"It's a great script. Once Paolan's done with it, it will be like everything else. It's a good thing I sold it today."

"You *sold* it?"

"Sure."

"How?"

I smile. It feels good to be on my way out. "I own the copyright. Paolan told me I should do whatever I need to protect myself. Since he pitched me a general idea and I wrote everything else from scratch, I thought safeguarding my work was the best way to go. I'm surprised you didn't suggest I do the same."

"I didn't think of it."

"You would if you represented me instead of Paolan's interests."

"Hey, I work for you, man."

"Come on. You're Paolan's *roommate*."

He straightens his posture, but I'm still taller than him. "Who did you sell it to?" he asks anxiously.

"The oligarch."

"Jesus."

"Don't worry. I know he's not going to make it. Thought I should be paid for my work, though."

"What a mess."

"It's not a mess. This game of you pretending to be my manager is a mess. But don't worry. I'll send you a check of your cut...and then I'll no longer require your services."

"Why don't we go back to the office to talk about this?"

"There's nothing to talk about. I'm moving back home."

Tighe takes a breath like he's fully aware of this development. Did he speak with the oligarch? "I can help you get your work seen," he says.

"You had plenty of time."

"Don't move home. It's a mistake."

"What do you know about my home?"

He takes a step toward me and says in a quiet voice, "Don't go home, man."

"What do you know about my home?"

"Enough to caution you. In fact, consider this an official warning," he says sheepishly. "From Raymond."

SEBASTIAN

2022

MY FIRST WORK trip is an exciting one. I grip the ticket in my right hand non-stop: Atlanta, 17A, window seat—a reassuring reminder of my upgraded position in the world. I'm now a performance consultant—one of the only ones I'm aware of. Possibilities for advancement are boundless. The job is what I make it.

On the plane, I sit down next to a college-age kid. He wears stylish glasses and carries an intrepid gaze. After we take off, he pulls a novel out of his briefcase and begins to read. It's Saul Bellow's *Seize the Day*. I recognize the text; I've seen Carson reading it—maybe when we were in college. Would like to begin a conversation. See what this guy would think of my new position.

"You like the book so far?" I ask.

He looks up, a little surprised. "Yeah, actually. The main character's really lost."

"Oh, yeah?"

"You read this before?"

"My twin brother has."

"Oh, you're a twin," he says, a little more interested. "That's cool. He like it?"

"Pretty sure he did."

"What's it like being a twin?"

I didn't expect this question. "Challenging," I say. "Especially if one of the twins is really talented."

"Is he the talented one?"

"How did you know?" I laugh.

He shrugs.

"I'm flying to a golf tournament."

"The Peachtree Invitational?" he says, taken aback.

"You bet."

"That's cool, man. What are you doing there?"

"I'm kind of a coach."

"What do you mean, you're *kind of* a coach?"

"It's a new kind of coach." I put some extra emphasis on the next phrase. "I'm a performance coach."

"Like acting?"

"Yeah."

"For a golfer?"

"Exactly," I say, pleased with myself.

"Which golfer?" he asks.

"Can't tell you."

"Probably a good idea."

"Why's that?"

"Well, it's not like you're an acting coach on some film or something. No one will expect a golfer to act. If you're coaching the guy, you probably don't want anyone to know he's acting. No one's expecting him to, right?" He smiles. He knows he made a smart observation, and it is. In fact, it kind of takes the sails out of everything a bit. If I can't tell people about my role, part of the excitement is ruined.

"That's a really good point."

"Sure," he says, like it's obvious. He turns his book to the back cover, like he's itching to begin reading again.

"May I ask what you're majoring in?" I inquire.

"American Studies." He squints like he's not entirely sure of his decision, even though he's likely past the point of no return. "I'll figure out something to do with it," he says, almost apologetically. Me, I've struggled from the day I graduated to settle on a career path. I envy this kid. He might pretend he's dangling in the dark, but the deliberate way he studies his text says better. Does Carson encounter the steady dread, the ominous uncertainty arising out of the ether, a personalized plague for one? Or does his abstract ability—this indecipherable secret dominion he supposedly taps into—shield him from the silent shock, the tiresome terror, because Mother believes he's special?

I lean back in my seat and try my hardest to center myself. Plenty to gain from my new position even if it's shrouded in secrecy. So what if I cannot reveal my role to the casual observer? Instead, I'll think of it more as an undercover operation. Close my eyes, the dread dissipating slightly, content once again.

As we descend, I observe the skyline of Atlanta materialize like a lost city suddenly found. Conifer trees lead to a crispness and modernity, replacing the relaxed muddle of the Parish. My seatmate continues to read his book, and I start to formulate my plan of attack upon landing. It's over an hour's drive to Macon. Will have to study the layout of the country club and the course. Time poses the largest obstacle. My return trip is tomorrow night. Hopefully Mackadoo holds an early tee time the next morning. I can tell everyone he wanted to employ my services for the first two rounds. I only have one night in the hotel. No one's going to see the hotel receipts, so my lodging location shouldn't set off any alarm bells. I nod at my seatmate and project a knowing air as we begin our final descent into the city.

There are steel bars on the front of the hotel, but online, the inside looked fairly classy for three stars. I enter the lobby to find a modern décor and the scent of rotten chestnuts. The room is compact, yet clean. Supposedly, there's a well-rated restaurant on the first floor, a total necessity and the reason why I selected this place. After dropping off my luggage, I head downstairs for some lunch. Only a few patrons in the dining room: a few single business guys and one family with two toddler-age kids. Take a seat by the window, which overlooks an industrial building. A street cleaning machine bustles past. Can hear the high-pitched hum through the window. A waitress with olive eyes and a surly demeanor greets me in a perfunctory way, drops a menu at my place setting. When she returns, I smile and point to my choice like a five-year-old.

"How's the BLT?" I ask.

"It's a BLT."

"Can you toast it?"

"Yeah, we can toast it."

"I'm here for the Peachtree Invitational. I'm a golf coach."

She looks at me skeptically. "Shouldn't you be heading there?"

"Wanted to try your lunch."

She nods, not sure what to make of me. She picks up my menu and walks away.

I look out the window again. The street cleaning machine's gone; the sidewalk less grimy. I am that street: even with the cleaning chemicals and swirling brushes sweeping across the pavement, there's still a sticky substance underneath that the brushes will never reach. Glance at the door to the kitchen. No sign of the waitress. Why am I always alone? I mean, obviously, my solitary state is a necessity today. This excursion should be an adventure, but how can it be when each passing moment, I plunge further toward some unknown abyss? Even if I wanted to, I couldn't go back now. The waitress returns with the sandwich and a side of coleslaw. The bacon is fresh and crisp, a dash of nourishment. I return to the semi-claustrophobic, yet ultimately satisfactory hotel room. Collapse on the bed and drift into a less panicked malaise, which turns into an unwitting slumber.

A rush to my forehead as my eyes open. It's six. On my way downstairs, I wish I could stay in the elevator longer, consider riding to the top before heading to the restaurant. They said the skyline view is stellar on the 15th floor, but I'd have to pretend to find it enjoyable. Would rather focus on dinner. A distinctive lighting fills the lonely dining room, making it urbane and even mysterious. I express my appreciation for their efforts by ordering a drink. I ask the waitress what girly drinks they have. She doesn't laugh. It's the same waitress from earlier. "Aren't you supposed to be in Macon?" she asks.

"Decided to go in tomorrow."

"Your guy didn't play today?"

"We talked on the phone."

"Sure," she says in a put-off tone.

"Tomorrow's the bigger day."

She brightens. "You feeling all right?"

"I'm all right. Thanks for asking."

"I'm not flirting with you, sir."

"Right—I know that."

"I'll come back," she says, though she doesn't. Instead, I get someone new, a shaggy-haired, college-age waiter with a superficial edge. "Can I get you something?" he asks, as if my presence in the restaurant is now some burden. What I thought was a conversation with the waitress is now a matter that needs "attending to." My friendliness might have aroused ill will. He brings me my hamburger. I chew in silence. The waitress passes me a few times but doesn't make eye contact. Spending time alone in public is overrated for sure. It's like going to the prom without a date. You can do it and enjoy some of the facets of the party, but after a while, you feel the prolonged looks and sense the suppressed sympathy. The waiter places my check on the table. He gives me a questioning look.

"Is this check correct?" he asks.

"You mean the bill?"

"I mean your name."

"Yeah. Is something wrong with my Visa?"

He shakes his head. "Your Visa card's fine."

I strain my neck to catch a glimpse of the waiter after he leaves, but he's gone already. I pay and head upstairs, settled on the decision I'll grab a bagel or something at the airport in the morning. In the hotel room, I purchase Bellow's *Seize the Day* on my Kindle and begin reading. I empathize with the strained relationship the main character has with his father. Reminds me of my relationship with both my parents. I peruse an online edition of *Golf Digest* before turning in, and resolve to sign up for a subscription when I return home so I can gather further details about this new world I'm involved in.

At one in the morning, I sit up sharply. A loud knock. Did I lock the chain? I believe I did. Swing my body off the bed. My feet pounce on the sticky carpet. Rush to the door; move my eye to the keyhole. No one's visible. Cannot resist and foolishly unlatch the door. Stick my head out. I'm shoved back in the room by sheer force. Someone's got a firm grip on my nightshirt. It's a girl. The waitress. She slams the door behind her.

"Hey, sorry for earlier," I say, somehow not quite noticing she's forced herself into my hotel room.

"Shut up," she says. She's strong; leans into me, managing to propel me toward the bed.

It's a challenge not to visibly acknowledge where she's pushed me and where she's standing. I should be concerned for my safety. Instead, against my better judgment, I'm aroused. I try to act casual despite the obvious burst of violence. "I don't have any money," I say.

"I don't want your money." She snatches my button-down off the recliner and tosses it at me. "Get dressed."

"Why?"

"You're Sebastian Levinson, right?"

I nod.

"Yeah, get dressed."

We take the stairs straight to the basement parking lot. I expect to find her car there, but instead we leave the hotel premises out a side door and head for the MARTA station. The inside of our subway car is peppered with candy wrappers and wet plastic bags. We sit across from each other. The air conditioning blows directly on her dirty golden hair. "You didn't tell me your name," I say.

"I know."

"I'd rather not call you waitress."

"Please don't." Finally, a resigned smile sneaks across her face. "It's Kirsten."

"Are you kidnapping me, Kirsten?"

"You followed me on the subway, bud."

"Am I in danger?"

"If anything, I'm in danger. For what I just did to you." We ride in silence the rest of the way. A smarter person would ask more, but I welcome the special attention and find it strangely comforting. Keep my eyes trained on her bare knees.

We ascend the stairs to deserted streets. Specks of moonlight illuminate the city sidewalk as we walk toward Centennial Olympic Park. Inside the park, we cross the old Olympic rings and head for the pond. "What are we doing in the park?" I ask. And then I see it. Quiet flames flicker from a fierce fire pit next to a clump of limestone. The glow from the flames lights up the magnolia trees like a birthday candle. The waiter from dinner emerges along with a Black man in his late thirties with penetrating indigo eyes. "Welcome," the man says. "You're Sebastian Levinson, are you not?"

"I told you that's his name," the waiter says.

"I want to hear it from him," the man says.

I look to Kirsten. "Yes, I'm Sebastian Levinson."

The man nods, a little relieved. "Let's go inside." He pushes one of the limestones downward, causing a steel grate to open a few feet from us. Steps emerge, leading into the earth. "That's not the sewer?" I ask.

"Come on," he says.

I follow them, leaving the park behind as we descend the steps into an unknown void. The man pulls a lever from the wall; a walkway extends outward. We take the walkway through a winding corridor. The damp air cuts through my lungs. Up ahead I see what looks to be furniture. A modern-looking kitchen table sits alongside two cedar bookcases, where thick, dusty, hardcovers line the shelves. A few overhead lamps lighten our faces in a soft glow. We take a seat on stools surrounding the table. "You're here for one thing," the man says. "I'm sure you know what that is."

I look at Kirsten. "I have no idea why I'm here."

The man chuckles. "To teach us how to heal."

"What?" I look again to Kirsten, expecting some kind of clarification she has no intention of providing. "I'm not religious."

"Not that kind of healing." He gestures at the waiter. "This is my colleague, Lawrence. He has an opioid addiction."

Lawrence recoils. "Unbelievable. You know I'm fine."

The man puts his hands up. "You're so beyond fine you forgot what it looks like." He gestures at me. "This guy holds the power we're looking for."

"What power?" I ask.

Kirsten glances at them, then at me. "You're Sebastian Levinson, are you not?"

"Yes."

"Of Orleans Parish?" the man adds. He waits 'til my eyes meet his. "The Society," he clarifies. "Of Orleans Parish."

"My parents," I say automatically.

"And you," the man says.

"We heard you're a healer," Kirsten says with a trace of frustration in her voice.

"From whom?"

"Don't intrude. Instead, you play by our rules," the man says.

The man's voice is like a stream, shaped by the ebbs and flows of his confidence. He commands the space as if he's excavated every corner and crevice. I envy him. If I could accomplish what he wants me to, I would. His belief in me nearly makes his hopes attainable. "I don't have it," I say.

"Have what?" Kirsten asks.

"Any ability."

"Nonsense," the man says.

I look at him like he's speaking another language.

Lawrence sulks away, imperceptible in the darkness. His voice leaves a trail behind him. "You screwed up, Gilliam."

"Your mother is Moira Levinson," Kirsten says with annoyance.

"Moira's my mother, but I can't do anything, do you hear? No ability!"

This man, Gilliam—his demeanor changes. He grits his teeth. His eyes grab hold of me. He produces a knife so fast all I see is the blade in the dim light. "Getting tired of this misdirection," he says. "You're probably wondering where's the rest of them. Where's our other members? Well, a lot of them perished in the Civil War before there was time to procreate. Glad they ran out of time. We had no use for them. 'Cause nobody wanted their racist ass progeny messing any further with the lifeblood of our city. So, our little coterie, our humble society had to start from scratch, you see. We know there's much to change, much we can do to transform this place for the better. But we lack the infrastructure y'all have in Orleans Parish. There's not enough of us yet with the right abilities. Some of those abilities can be learned." He lets go of the knife. It stays floating in the air as if someone's still holding it steady. "You show us how you heal." The knife glides toward Kirsten. "Then we'll take you back to your hotel."

The knife stops an inch away from Kirsten's arm. She regards me. I can sense there's a different kind of wound there: constant. I'd like to place my palm on her stomach, wash the festering ache away. My own intuition tells me it's there, but as much as I wish to alleviate her pain, I lack the know-how.

"He can't do it, Gilliam," she says. "Don't be foolish."

"I want to," I say.

"But you can't," she says.

The knife hovers in my direction. My face lowers to the floor, defeated. The knife drops, makes a clanging rattle. An older African American gentleman emerges from the same vacuous space the waiter escaped to. His authority is calmer than Gilliam. His gray eyes fill the entire room with veiled conviction. "You have the wrong man," he says.

Gilliam gazes at the knife lying on the dirty ground.

"You have his twin brother," the older gentleman says.

Gilliam glares at me. "He has a twin?"

The gentleman looks at me thoughtfully. "One of them is blessed. This is not the one."

CARSON

2022

A CAB CARRIES me from the airport into the outskirts of Kenner, guiding me past trailer parks and run-down gas stations, which loiter along the service road like schoolyard bullies. We sneak onto the 10, and the heavy scent of wet vegetation takes over. I see the outline of the Parish come into view. Steal a glance toward the decaying cemetery to my right. Did these souls spend their whole lives here? Or did they return after a failed exodus? Were they missing something only attainable among the bermudagrass and stale scents of solemn alcohol? As Jefferson Parish falls away, I'm unsure what to expect. Brace myself for whatever Mom was protecting me from. The harried sparkle of the Superdome peeks its bulbous head out. Closer now than I wish to ponder.

And then I feel it. Not all at once—first a subtle push against my knee like I've unexpectedly slipped inside a hot tub, a flash of heat rising through my veins, oscillating to a royal flush. My vision sharpens but not to what's in front. Instead I see intention. Beyond. Beyond the cab, beyond the highway—I'm a magnifying glass unsure where to direct my attention. This is Orleans

Parish. Don't want to give in; it's more powerful than anything in LA. Here it comes from all directions, infiltrating the senses. Assembling a clarion call for me to listen—to the earth, to the ghosts of the Parish long past.

And then I relax. I allow it to permeate. It gives way to my emotions. And his. I sense his desperation. His need to impress, his burning desire to be more than he could possibly ever accomplish—to be more than me. I never wanted to play such a game. If I came off that way, it was my mistake. Listen. Pull back, I want to tell him. Why are you with her? Do you realize what she's capable of? You're sledding down the hill, and the blade's about to snap. Sebastian's in danger.

ADDISON

2022

WE'RE IN MY apartment, where he refuses to discuss his trip to Atlanta. "What's Mackadoo like?" I ask him.

"Professional," he says. "With a quiet confidence. It's infectious."

"Sounds fun," I say, not meaning it. I'm at the kitchen counter chopping onions for a salad. Sebastian watches for a while, silent and brooding. I prefer to avoid starting a new conversation while I chop, yet the lack of discussion makes me feel like we're not really clicking. If he made himself useful, I might consider flirting. If he took some initiative, I might display some affection. He walks up behind me; watch out—he's on the prowl. Feel his arms come together around my waist: pasty sensation like an intruder. My body tightens; I shift away from him. "Let me finish cutting," I say, trying my hardest not to sound patronizing.

After dinner, we comb through the streaming service, searching for a movie to watch. We settle on an old Judd Apatow film. A girl meets a guy. They sleep together. She calls an Uber after. His cell phone rings. It's him. He's the Uber driver. It goes on from there.

Sebastian laughs. "I've never been in an Uber."

No laugh from me. "That's not funny."

"What?"

"That you've never taken an Uber. Why not?"

"I haven't left the Parish in a long time. Where would I have the opportunity to."

"You were in Atlanta last week."

"Oh, right." He makes a weird face.

"We're taking an Uber tomorrow to the airport."

"Why?"

"Because I can't believe you've never been in one."

"It's just some guy's car. I didn't know it was special."

I place my hand on his thigh against my better judgment. His torso grows rigid.

"We already have a car service to take us to the airport," he says.

"So we'll cancel it. For an Uber." He's a hair away from sulking. "What?" I ask.

Can see he's being careful with his words as if the wrong combination will set off a fire alarm. "It doesn't concern you?" he says. "The fact that Ubers are driven by strangers. From a safety perspective."

"It doesn't. Are you afraid, Sebastian?"

"I'm not afraid," he says defensively.

"Good. I'll book the Uber tomorrow."

"Fine," he says.

I turn off the TV. "I don't want to watch this movie anymore."

"You don't?"

I say nothing. I still have my hand on his thigh.

"What do you want to do?"

"What do *you* want to do?"

He looks down at my hand.

I take his hand in mine, lead him to my bedroom.

In the bedroom, I light a coconut beach candle. Remain cognizant not to make the room redolent of older scents, scents from my beautiful creature. We kiss. It's nice for a while. He's an above-average kisser, which I knew before. My clumsy hand finds its way to his damp stomach. Grab a strand of his dark chest hair underneath his shirt. His heart races. Not in a good way. Makes me nervous. I read him. He's on a different frequency—an apprehensive one. Nothing's going to happen. I can sense this before we even try. So I don't bother. I leave him on the bed. Stride to the kitchen. Spend the night on the couch in the living room. I lock the hallway divider; keep him quarantined in the bedroom area. He has access to my bathroom. I do not feel guilty about it.

In the morning, an aroma of breakfast eggs mixed with tiny slices of ham wafts through the bright kitchen. Hallway divider's unlocked. When he enters, I do not talk about it. I won't talk about it. He sits and smiles at me, stupidly. We eat in silence. I'm glad he's dressed. Wouldn't want to have to tell him to get ready for the airport. Not my job. He's nervous. You can tell from his speech, a diffident tone, almost yearning to move back in time. Difficult to discern if his reticence is because of last night or the impending Uber ride. I decide to book the Uber in front of him. Pull out my smartphone. It's done. On the way. I grin, rather satisfied. I cannot stand irrationality.

In the car, he tries to hold my hand on the way to the airport. I say "tries." Move my hand away. This throws him off. He stares at the Uber driver, who looks no older than twenty with long-unkept red hair. Sebastian exhales. Releases a sulking sound. Look out the window. The air conditioning churns at half capacity. The perspiration soaks through the back of my shirt. When we turn onto Highway 10, I take Sebastian's hand. He releases his facials muscles, relieved. He shouldn't be.

The plane lifts off the runway. The homes of Kenner look like weathered gingerbread houses from above. As we turn from the Parish, I can see the once repaired but now deteriorating levee, overrun when a major hurricane touched down at the beginning of the century.

"The levee's going to crumble," Sebastian says unexpectedly.

"When?"

"As soon as the next hurricane arrives."

"We'll have to deal with it then."

"My father designed an awesome one."

"I heard that."

"Too bad your uncle prevented him from building it."

"That's not what happened."

Sebastian nudges me playfully. "Of course it is."

I notice his bushy eyebrows for the first time. They're more attractive than at first glance.

"My uncle has to be careful what changes he allows. It can cause repercussions within other aspects of the city."

"You mean other businesses. That The Society controls."

"I'd rather not talk about it."

"You brought it up."

"Actually you brought it up, Sebastian."

He looks at me. "Are you going to take over someday?"

"I'd rather not discuss that either."

"Do you want to take over?"

I turn away from him in a huff and look out the window.

"Not a denial," I hear him say. A moment of silence. "What's your power?"

I shake my head. I imagine there are advantages to making a life with someone without abilities. Would be nice to avoid the ever-constant competition.

The air outside West Palm Beach Airport is a blow dryer to the face, churning gusts of hot steam. It's a relaxing change from the stalking humidity of the Parish, and I'm even more upbeat once we're on the way to the golf course in our second Uber of the day. Sebastian leans into me, never taking his eyes off the driver. We reach the resort grounds in Juno Beach, a sprawling apparatus on a crescent of land facing a composed ocean. We leave our bags at the front desk and head for the first hole.

"Are you going to coach him before the round?" I ask.

"I already spoke to him on the phone."

"When?" I ask, surprised. "You've been with me the whole day."

"Not when you were in the bathroom."

"Are we going to meet him after?"

He leads me around the spectators with confidence, which reassures me he's in familiar territory. "It depends how long it takes him to finish the round."

"Why?"

"He'll have some interviews afterwards."

"Shouldn't you be there for that?"

"We covered it all on the phone."

Sebastian takes my hand; we maneuver around a throng of middle-aged men in pastel polos and shorts too tight for their own good. We scurry along the barrier set up on the outer part of the fairway. I've never seen this Skip Mackadoo on television, so I'm relieved when we catch a glimpse of his assured persona fifty yards away as he walks toward the tee box on the second hole, a picturesque par-4, which bends along the beach below us. We watch him tee off while we stand near the putting green of the first hole. I notice his blonde hair hang out the open part of his baseball cap. He smacks his drive down the fairway. The guy really is charismatic. He flashes a mischievous grin to an attractive female onlooker as soon as his follow-through is complete, which he holds for an extra second. I whisper to Sebastian. "He has a nice smile."

"It's contagious, isn't it?"

"Did you two work on that?"

"A little," Sebastian says, proud.

"Hope we can meet him."

"Yeah, me too. Let's catch up to him."

Once we're almost in range to view the action up close, Sebastian trips over a rock perhaps, hiding in the grass. I give him my hand. "You okay?"

He looks up in pain. "May have sprained my ankle."

"Really?" He exaggerates. Mackadoo is almost to the green of the second hole while we're still only thirty yards from the tee box. "Can you walk?"

Sebastian nods unconvincingly. He rises and brushes the grass and dirt off his shorts. He takes my hand again. I consider leaving him behind and forging ahead now that he's moving like an elderly man with half the day to kill. A picnic bench is set up beyond the tee box. "Let's sit for a minute," he tells me. Mackadoo, along with his charisma, is on the putting green.

"We're going to lose him," I say, concerned.

"We can catch up."

I know we won't, though. I look at Sebastian. Something's wrong with this picture. Like first, how on earth did he trip in the rough? From what I know about golf, it's obvious this course is well-tended. Sebastian should be used to this environment even though he's just begun this new job.

Unless, of course, he hasn't. Would he *really*...? Why would he take me here, though, where Mackadoo is competing? The astronomical nerve it would require on Sebastian's part is unfathomable. But plausible. He lobs me one of those dumb smirks of his. Looks like the kind of guy who forgets his wallet at the movies and swears there was some kind of mix-up, so his friends have to pay. I observe the gray clouds sneaking in from the west, darkness descending on this serene resort where my future balances atop a spindle. I close my eyes. Sebastian doesn't even see me do it. I breathe. Feel the inside of the cloud, the soaking cake, expanding outward, ready to multiply to a thousand-fold when I give the word. I open my eyes. And give the word. Righteous rain. Unexpected and exact, assaulting the course from all angles—a slippery package striking golf carts, seven-irons, and any hopes of completing the round. Sebastian looks up at me, stunned. "We better get inside," I say. I place my arms in his. We scuffle toward the clubhouse. He takes a few steps faster than he should, at least according to the pain he's in. "Don't overdo it," I tell him. His disjointed steps divulge not an injury but an agitation, for Mackadoo approaches in our direction because of the hammering rain. My rain. Our hair is drenched. My shoes step through bubbles of moisture mixed in with the stiff grass. We're almost to the concrete pavement along the first tee when Mackadoo walks alongside us, the jumbo carrot-colored umbrella his caddy holds sheltering them both from the downpour.

And then Sebastian surprises me. With every bit of his strength, he raises his hand confidently in the air, gesturing to Mackadoo. "When you smiled at the crowd after your second drive, it had the perfect effect."

Mackadoo appears a little surprised—but only a little. He beams back at Sebastian. "Thanks, man."

I glare at this cocksure golfer. "We came all the way from Louisiana," I call out. He motions to his caddy; they stop. The jumbo umbrella holds steady.

He looks at me. "So glad you came."

Sebastian tips his head in a celebratory wink.

Mackadoo, pleased with the moment, steps toward the clubhouse, the caddy following. "Nice to see you both," he says, but keeps an eye on me.

I stand in place. Knees bent. Going nowhere. Sebastian notes my firm stance in the sopping wetness. He comes closer. Avoids my eyes. *Time for you to say something, young man.*

"Isn't he nice?" Sebastian asks with boisterous, assertive vigor. Does he believe he's gotten away with it?

"Nice?" I say in disbelief.

He regards me. Picks up a lone golf tee he sees in the soggy grass. Rubs it between his thumb and forefinger.

"Don't make me ask you." We say nothing for a long moment as the rain continues to thump.

"I don't know him," he finally says.

"Go on."

"I met him once. At Audubon. I thought it would be a neat job."

"You pretended?"

He grips the tee in his other hand.

"Do you still work at the school?"

He shakes his head.

"Why?"

"I took this job instead."

"This was never a job!"

"Okay, I was fired."

I nod, attempting to process it all. "Come on; let's go," I say.

We pass the tee box. The driving range. The clubhouse. It continues to pour. Once you start something, there is no stopping. Made up my mind. "Let's walk to the ocean," I say. We descend a series of winding steps. The wind blows misty sand at our feet. Rainfall clears the beach: only us. He's unusually serene. My hand takes his and when I do, I feel Carson as well. He's returned to the Parish. The dirt, the buildings, the Quarter: they've inundated him. He has no idea what he's waiting for. I look up at poor, clueless Sebastian. No need for you to be your brother. If only you knew the advantages of being normal. "Just kiss me," I tell him. He leans in. Sweet— then deep. His soft tongue finds my own. My arms wrap around his waist. Hands slip under his shirt. Press firmly. Then a little more. Tighter. Tighter still. "You want to know what I can do?" I whisper.

He nods.

"I helped it rain."

His eyes roll, arrogantly.

"It was me just now. Passing the rain along." He thinks. See the understanding behind his eyelids. Does he realize the implications? Think he does. In case he doesn't, I tell him. "I wanted to see how you and Mackadoo would react." His lips purse. "Also I can do this." I press. Press harder—underneath his shirt. Slippery skin of his belly. Soft on the outside. Then watery. Blood. Membrane-like. He recoils. Press harder. You can see it on my face. And his. I'm inside him. Maneuvering the cartilage. More blood. Pull a strand—out the other end. See the gooey tissue drip off my sticky hand. He falls. Head in the sand. Flat...finished.

MOIRA

⁙⸻⸺⸻⸙⸻⸺⸻⸙

2022

IT'S ONE OF those nights. Feel it in the ether. In the starlight scrutinizing the Mississippi. Know I'll look back on tonight with regret but also with appreciation, for I can feel the dissolution of the status quo, emerging in the shadows, rearing for a fight. Scents of fine perfumes, hair straightener, and too much starch permeate the dark suits and black dresses, the patterned shirts, which plead for attention. We sit at a quiet table, Victor and I, bathed in soothing cream candlelight. Our table is only one of seventy scattered about: couples willing themselves to drink the Kool-Aid once again, soothing it down with gin and bourbon.

Sebastian does not answer my texts. He has no invitation to this event, though he certainly could have accompanied Addison as her guest had she invited him. I question her decision not to. She sits on the stage next to Raymond. Her silver necklace glitters around her neck. The phone rests on our metallic tabletop waiting for Sebastian's signal. Victor glances at it from time to time; as usual, he's not as concerned as I am. I watch Addison, waiting for her to acknowledge my focused glances to no avail. At two minutes to eight, the phone lights up in eerie green. Glance at Victor as I snatch it. Hopeful relief shifts to unadulterated trepidation when I see Carson's name instead of Sebastian's. On the way? How close? He discussed his plans to return temporarily but not this soon. Not here. I hand the phone to Victor. He's amused. "Let him try to get inside. They probably won't even let him in."

"You're not worried?"

"I'm confident Sebastian's fine."

Raymond takes the stage. The crevices around his eyes give way to a fragileness I've never noticed before. Runs his hands through his soft white hair and, unlike his niece, manages to make eye contact with me. Slips in a glimmer of a smile. Seems resigned to some decision he made a while back that's now unfolding in front of him as if he had nothing to do with it. He picks up a microphone. He taps it and the hollow bounce of an echo emanates throughout the ballroom. "Welcome to our annual gathering," he says with careful authority. A serene Addison watches Raymond with agile eyes. "I will begin with an announcement many years in the making," he says. "One year from now, Addison Liondale will succeed me." A few gasps. They fall away to a steady stream of clapping, louder than I'm comfortable with. Addison grins like a long-distance runner, surprised to see the finish line materialize earlier than expected.

Check the phone again to see if Sebastian texted. Nothing.

"As is customary," Raymond continues, "if anyone would like to nominate a different person, the gesture is certainly welcome." It isn't, of course, and now Addison glowers at me, finally acknowledging my presence for the first time this evening.

"Want to place your name in?" Victor asks under his breath.

"No, thank you."

The soles of a man's dress shoe impart a steady, upbeat clapping sound against the tiled floor. Raymond spots Carson, who makes his way toward the stage. "Excuse me," Raymond says. "You're not permitted to be here."

Carson shakes a little when he speaks. "I have some business, which concerns everyone."

"You need to be a member to consult the congregation," Raymond says.

"Make an exception."

"I know you, Carson. You chose to walk away from the Parish. You cannot simply return when you feel like it." Raymond gestures at two men in gray suits near the stage. Their muscles flex through their dress shirts. Never seen them before. They approach Carson.

I sit up in my seat, ready to lunge. Victor places his hand on my arm. "Wait," he says.

Carson looks at his own hand like a brand-new baseball glove in his grasp. He gestures at the two men. A brilliant pulsation of plum-colored energy escapes from his hand, knocking them backward onto the floor. Several men rise from their tables, ready to defend Raymond against my son, the unknown assailant. Carson pivots around two tables. Never seen him this fast—a falcon, charging toward the stage. He leaps up the steps, planting himself ten feet from Addison, who moves to protect Raymond.

Carson turns to us all, keeping his hand aimed at

Addison. "As soon as I arrived in the Parish, I sensed it. Can you? Check the atmosphere. My twin brother, Sebastian Levinson, is missing. Where is he?"

"Back away," Addison says.

"Close your eyes and search," he says to us all. "Can you see him?"

"Get off the stage," she shouts.

"You cannot see him. Because he isn't missing." Carson gestures at Addison. "He's dead, isn't he? And you killed him."

She attempts a laugh. "I did no such thing."

"Where is he then?"

"My apartment."

I look at my cell phone, useless on the table.

"What did he do to you? What drove you to it?"

Raymond frowns; he's concerned now.

Glance at Victor. There's our Carson, all grown up, on the stage, ready to fight for his brother. Search for my baby. Past the oak trees. Across the crumbling levee. Through the bog water filled with oil and tar. Nothing. Cannot feel him. Little boy. My lost little boy. I placed him in the killer's hands. Watch myself spring from my seat; confront the gray-suited men, who fall like petite toy dolls at my lightening hands. An angry pulse releases, shining orange, hurdling toward Addison before she can make an excuse, before additional subterfuge.

But she somehow slows everything, shifts her body ever so slightly to the right so the pulse smacks into Raymond, knocking him to the floor. I recoil. Addison, who should tend to her fallen uncle, takes the opportunity to smack Carson in the face. Carson grabs her around the waist; he pulls her toward him, then spins her outward at the audience. "Go ahead and tell them. It's against your laws to kill one of your own."

She glares back at Carson before releasing an errant pulse at him. "Your brother's not a member."

I run to Raymond. Feel his forehead. Still breathing.

"My uncle's weak," she says. She looks out at all the guests. "You've been biding your time. Tending old gardens. Well, I can do better. I will bring prosperity to the Parish. For all of us." A hypnotic stillness. The members mull it over in their selfish heads. A group of men stand first. Of course they do. Followed by their wives. Of course they do too. See their pearls shimmer in the shadow of the stage light. More stand. But not everyone. Some watch Carson. They wait for him.

Addison giggles, enjoying the moment she's no doubt waited for. "You don't want this, Carson. There's no need to be stupid just because your brother was. You were in LA for a reason; you should have stayed there."

"I was away too long," he says.

Addison displays her teeth. "Not long enough. Believe me, you were better off with your stories and the movie stars. We'll deal with the real issues."

Carson glances at me and Raymond, then at his own hands. He feels her out, waiting for his next chance to strike. In the meantime, he asks the standing crowd, "You really want to be led by her?"

Some are indecisive. Too many are all in.

My surviving son does one last unexpected thing. He tells them calmly, "If you want to follow her, be prepared to deal with the outside. I'm going to find my brother's body. Then I will turn her in. Anyone who sticks by her be warned. Your current ways are unsustainable." He points at Raymond. "That man wanted me away from the Parish." Addison shoots a pulse at him. He dodges it. "I see why," he says. He lunges toward her. She shatters the glass window, slipping out of it.

Along the anxious streetcar tracks and the lazy waves of the Mississippi, the Parish waits patiently, anticipating when to show me something unfamiliar. From Uptown to the Quarter, between the living and the non, our abilities drift through everything before us and among everything still to come. I believed no good would result from coarse traditions. Only more corruption and graft, and unadorned dominance. But something's different now. Something I never believed I'd see. Too many emotions to simply feel just one. They each surround me like little burning stars. Up here on the stage, cannot access the feelings I need to release for Sebastian. Otherwise I'll expire too. Must wait till it's safe to mourn. In the meantime, a moral leader emerges in front of the room.

My son.

ABOUT ATMOSPHERE PRESS

Atmosphere Press is an independent, full-service publisher for excellent books in all genres and for all audiences. Learn more about what we do at atmospherepress.com.

We encourage you to check out some of Atmosphere's latest releases, which are available at Amazon.com and via order from your local bookstore:

Queen of Crows, a novel by S.L. Wilton

The Summer Festival is Murder, a novel by Jill M. Lyon

Swimming with the Angels, a novel by Colin Kersey

Island of Dead Gods, a novel by Verena Mahlow

Cloakers, a novel by Alexandra Lapointe

Twins Daze, a novel by Jerry Petersen

Embargo on Hope, a novel by Justin Doyle

Abaddon Illusion, a novel by Lindsey Bakken

Melancholy Vision: A Revolution Series Novel, by L.C. Hamilton

Voodoo Hideaway, a novel by Vance Cariaga

ABOUT THE AUTHOR

Chad Pentler is the author of the plays, *Mind Your Offspring* and "Your Very Own Daughter." He was a screenwriter in Los Angeles and now teaches high school English. He received his M.F.A. in Dramatic Writing from Carnegie Mellon University and an M.Phil. from Trinity College, Dublin. He attended Tulane University for college, in Orleans Parish. He lives in Boca Raton, Florida. This is his first novel.